107 —

VILLAGE
OF
OUTCASTS

By the Same Author: *Pulga*

VILLAGE OF OUTCASTS

S. R. VAN ITERSON

Translation from the Dutch
by Patricia Pitzele and Joske Smedts

William Morrow and Company   New York

For Bernhard, Foyita, and Nora Helena

VILLAGE
OF
OUTCASTS

1

He could hear them talking as he sat huddled between the piles of sacks under the overhanging roof. They could not see him at all on this side of the house, where the wind blew from the mountains, yet he was very close to them. Their words reached him clearly, but he did not understand what they were talking about. He knew, though, that it concerned him.

"Yes, it's better," said Rafael again.

"It's better," repeated Don Pacho. He did not sound convinced.

"There's no one," Rafael continued, "to take care of you anymore. Lucila is busy enough as it is."

"Yes, it's true. Lucila is busy," the old man agreed. "And Sonia, my wife, may she rest in peace." He crossed himself.

"Lucila is busy," Rafael said, as though he had not heard Don Pacho. "With this big house, all the children, the cooking for the family, and the livestock: the chickens, the turkeys, the sheep."

"Ah, the turkeys and the sheep," the old man echoed, his tone sad. "I'm the one who always. . . ."

"But now you can't anymore," interrupted Rafael.

"No, not anymore," conceded Don Pacho.

"It's better that you go there," said Rafael, returning to the point.

"Yes."

"And eleven pesos." Rafael's voice underlined the words. "Just think, eleven pesos a day, without doing anything for it."

"Eleven pesos?" Don Pacho did not sound impressed. Never in his life had he experienced doing nothing and getting paid for it.

"And Claudio is going with you, after all."

"Claudio is going with me, yes. I wouldn't want to take the trip alone. It is far, and I am not as young as I was." He sighed. "Here in Boyacá I know every village, every lane. I've never been down there. Never. Who would think . . . Virgen Santa. . . ." The old man shook his head as anxiety swept over him. He sniffed and spat through the open door onto the cement floor outside.

"Hm," muttered Lucila in disapproval, as she entered the room, one child in her arms and two holding her skirt. She was a tall, angular woman, older than her husband. Her full lips gave her face a stupid appearance, but her narrowed, slanting eyes were sly, her expression sullen. She looked at her husband.

"It's all settled. Father is going," Rafael said quickly. "It's better for him, isn't it, Father?"

Don Pacho glanced at his daughter-in-law. "Yes," he said.

Lucila's face didn't change expression. Her eyes went from Rafael to the old man, and then down to the children clinging to her skirt. She hoisted the baby higher on her arm. "If my father-in-law wants it so," she said.

"It will be strange," Don Pacho muttered. "For years I've lived here in my own home. And now to go away all of a sudden, all alone. . . ."

"But you're going with Claudio," interrupted his son.

"Oh yes, with Claudio. I'm going with Claudio," the old man said, repeating the words as if to reassure himself.

Among the sacks Claudio stirred uneasily. Where was he supposed to go with his father? He must find out. Yet he did not dare go inside and ask them. Instead, he slipped away and headed for the village, where his half-sister Helena lived. Perhaps she knew what was happening. Helena was the oldest, older even than Rafael, and if the problem concerned Lucila in some way, Helena certainly would tell him! Helena and Lucila did not like each other. In fact, they hated each other. Yes, he would go to Helena.

It was cold. The sun, which at midday had burned

fiercely, was dipping behind the mountains. A bleak wind blew ragged gray rainclouds across the fields. He would have to hurry or he would get soaked. Suddenly Claudio caught sight of his brother Gerardo in a last ray of sunlight, driving his herd of cattle over the hill toward the corral beyond the house. Claudio changed his mind and decided to ask him instead.

Like Rafael, Gerardo was Claudio's half-brother, but Claudio liked him better. Rafael was a son of Don Pacho's first marriage, Gerardo was the youngest son of the second marriage, and Claudio the only child of the last marriage. Just four years apart, he and Gerardo always had played together and gone to school together until Rafael, or rather Lucila, said that Gerardo must start working on the *finca*.

Yes, Gerardo, who still lived with the family at home, was more likely to know what was going on than Helena, who lived down in the village. "Gerardo," Claudio shouted.

Gerardo looked up. Seeing Claudio race toward him, he reined in his horse. "What's the matter?" he asked.

"Do you know where we're going?" puffed Claudio, out of breath.

"Who?"

"Why, Father and I. . . ." Claudio was not sure how to proceed.

"How should I know, Claudio?" Gerardo looked away over the broad, rocking backs of the cows.

"You do know. I heard Rafael mention it to you."
Claudio watched Gerardo sharply. He made a lucky
guess.

"Well," Gerardo began slowly. "It's difficult to say
exactly. Maybe you're going to Bogotá."

Claudio's mouth fell open. To Bogotá! He never had
dreamed of going there. "To Bogotá!" he repeated,
trying to grasp the idea. "You really think that's
where we're going?" His eyes glowed as he remembered María's tales of the city. María was Rafael's
sister and a schoolteacher in Bogotá.

The city was fabulous. It had movie theaters, bars,
music, and stores that sold many things. At night everything was lighted up brightly. María did not de-
scribe it that way, but from the disapproving frown
with which she talked about Bogotá, Claudio understood that a lot went on there.

"Are you *sure* that's where we're going?" he asked
again.

"Maybe yes, maybe no." Gerardo was not helpful.

Claudio was silent. Again he was aware of a vague
sense of apprehension, the same threatening feeling he
had experienced when overhearing the conversation
between his brother and his father. Something was
going on that he did not trust. He pondered how to
provoke Gerardo into saying more. Suddenly Claudio
remembered one of the things that had been said.

"Is it true, you get eleven pesos a day there?" he
asked.

"Yes, if you register."

"Me, too?"

"Only if you're ill," Gerardo replied. "It's eleven pesos a day if you're ill. Can you imagine? That's more than Rafael gives me. Ave María!"

"But how. . . ." Claudio was bewildered.

"Stop bothering me now," said his brother irritably. "Open the gate and put the animals inside."

The last rays of sunlight had disappeared. At the gate of the corral the cows jostled each other and mooed. Claudio did as he was told. He ran to open the gate, then threw lumps of earth at the cattle to drive them through. Gerardo rounded up the strays and, without waiting for his brother, rode toward the huge, delapidated house and disappeared inside.

When Claudio entered the large, cheerless room, Gerardo was already there, talking to Rafael. His other brothers and sisters stood around silently. Only Lucila was absent.

"Everything is settled. Father is going," Rafael was saying firmly. He noticed Claudio and added, "And you're going, too. To help him, do you hear?"

Claudio nodded. He wanted to ask if they were going to Bogotá, as Gerardo had said. Had he really meant it? Claudio was not sure.

Lucila came out of a bedroom, where she had just put the baby to sleep. "I'll get your things together," she told Claudio. "And your father's." She looked over at the old man in the chair, with two grandchildren at his knee.

Don Pacho paid no heed. He sat, legs astride, before the open door. His eyes lost in the distance, he leaned forward a little with his weight on the cane clasped between his misshapen hands. Apparently he could not gaze enough at the rolling hills, bleak beneath the gray clouds. He knew every foot of the hills and the valleys beyond. He knew every path: the steep tracks along the mountainside, the soggy footpaths across the *páramo*, the roads that fanned out toward the big haciendas through little villages hidden in the mountain folds. He knew it all, all of Boyacá and Ráquira too, where they journeyed in the old days to buy pottery for resale at nearby towns and village fairs. The old man sighed.

The children were still small then. Helena and Rafael and María and, yes, the twins who had died all had accompanied him, young as they were. But Gerardo and Claudio did not know Ráquira. Nor did his simpleminded Julia, the one with the crooked shoulder. Julia and Gerardo and Claudio were not born yet. Only the children from his first marriage to Elvira had been with him then. Elvira, his first wife, who had been so young and enchanting! "May she rest in peace," he murmured.

Don Pacho still could picture himself and the family taking the daylong trip through hills, across mountains, and driving the mules before them. Frequently other families had joined them along the road, friends and acquaintances from the villages around. The *páramo* they crossed to reach Ráquira always had been bitterly cold, without any shelter against the cutting wind. Usually it was misty, and often they were caught in a downpour. Later, in the inn near Jiritos where they spent the night, they sat together and drank *chicha*. The *chicha*, which was a fermented drink made from corn, had warmed them and appeased their hunger. Next day they descended into the sunny valley, at the other side of the *páramo*, to Ráquira, where they had known a lot of people. Together they sat around the market in the tiny shops, bought pottery, and drank more *chicha*.

Ah, he remembered that *chicha* was forbidden now. It had been forbidden for a long time, but one could still buy it if he knew where to go.

The years passed. After he married Lely, he had gone into the horse trading business with César, the cousin of his wife. César always had been the cousin of his wife, since Don Pacho had married three daughters, from the youngest to the oldest, in the same family.

"The girls from the house with the high hydrangeas" they had been called in the village. One day their mother confided to a neighbor that she was afraid her daughters never would find a husband.

"Cut down all the hydrangeas," the neighbor advised. "No one ever marries girls from a house with hydrangeas."

The mother didn't hesitate for a second and immediately uprooted all her handsome bushes.

Clearly the advice had helped. First Don Pacho had married Elvira, then Lely, and after Lely also died he married Sonia, the oldest. She was Claudio's mother and had been buried a month now. "May she rest in peace," he murmured.

On that day Don Pacho had seen César again. César had been present at every family funeral, even that of the twins.

The old man's meandering thoughts went back to the time when they had been in the horse trading business together. He smiled. Those days had been the best, and they had earned a lot. Certainly his large family had needed the money, for the new babies kept coming. Still, he had done well and was able to buy new, fertile land.

César had known the wealthy farmers while he, Pacho, was famous for his good hands with a horse. Nobody anywhere around could handle horses the way he did. Old ones that looked like bags of bones, he knew how to fatten up. Skittish young stallions he controlled with a finger. Mares long in the tooth became as lively as fiery Arabs when he rode them. Why, here at this very door he had sat when someone, who had bought a magnificent horse from him the day before, came to complain that the damned wretch did not budge.

"I sold you the horse, but not my legs," he had retorted. Aye, his legs, how they hurt him now. And his hands, all gnarled and out of shape. There were times, in the night especially, when everything hurt. Rheumatism, he told himself. Only it was not rheumatism, the doctor said. Uneasily Don Pacho moved his flat, worn-out feet, which were so painful now.

A grandchild stumbled heavily against the old man's knee. Absentmindedly he raised his clawlike hand and stroked her head. Still he stared outside, at the gathering dark and the rain sweeping in gusts over the land. His property was fertile, and the house sturdy and large. Perhaps it had become a little seedy and neglected over the years. Many children had played in the rooms, under the overhanging roof of the veranda, in the inner court with the geraniums. Now Rafael, his oldest son, had told him he must move away. When they heard what the doctor had to say, fear had swept over them. They were afraid of his illness; that was the truth. There was no place for him here, in his own house, anymore. "*Aca no esta mas su casa,*" Rafael had said to him. "This is not your house anymore."

2

Two days later they left.

Gerardo accompanied them as far as the main road where the bus passed. The day before Lucila had brushed her father-in-law's dark suit carefully and put it in the sun to air. Don Pacho had brought out his yellow leather shoes. They were the same shoes in which he had been married three times, but he hardly could put them on. The leather had become hard and stiff, and it had shrunk. Or maybe his feet had changed their shape over the years. Stubbornly he persisted. He would make the journey in his wedding shoes.

Claudio walked behind his father, the wooden box of clothes on one shoulder and a small, brown cardboard suitcase in his other hand.

Brothers and sisters, in-laws and little children, all were standing in the doorway, as if for a family picture, to watch them go. Lucila plucked nervously at her dress. Julia, with the crooked shoulder, started to sob. The other brothers and sisters stared straight ahead. Rafael moved uneasily. Then the little children began to cry too.

"Where is Papa-Pacho going?" asked the eldest girl loudly.

"Is he taking a trip?" questioned another.

"Be quiet, all of you," ordered Rafael. "Yes, your grandfather is going on a trip. He wanted it that way himself." After a short silence he added, "It's better this way."

"You . . . you gave him some money, didn't you?" Lucila asked hesitatingly. "How much did you give him?"

"Enough for the journey and a little extra. As soon as he's registered, he'll receive money there too. And Claudio is with him to take care of him. They'll manage."

"Yes, they'll manage," Lucila repeated. "It couldn't go on like this."

Nobody answered. They remained silent, standing in the doorway, watching the little procession until it disappeared between the hills and the cornfields.

Gerardo looked at his lagging father. "We'll have to hurry, or you'll miss the bus. The bus to Bogotá."

"Yes, yes," mumbled Don Pacho. He couldn't walk briskly anymore, and he leaned heavily on his stick.

At each hut that they passed, women and children came out to stare at them curiously. "Are you going away?" one would ask.

"Yes," answered Claudio.

"Where to?" asked another.

"To Bogotá in the bus."

"All of you or will you be on your own?"

"With my father." He saw the envy on their faces, and he straightened his back.

At the main road Helena was waiting for them. "Here," she said to Claudio. "This is for you." She put a new bright red sportshirt in the suitcase. "And this is for Father. Twelve handkerchiefs. White." She sniffed a few times and wiped her eyes.

"Poor thing," she said softly. "Poor thing. . . . It's a pity!"

"Hush," admonished Gerardo, looking nervously at his father, who sat down on the roadside. Don Pacho was gazing blankly into space. The walking had tired him, although it was not far from his house to the road. The shoes must be bothering him.

They sat together in silence. Gerardo kept his eye on the road. At last he said, "It's coming. There's the bus."

"Yes," said the old man, without looking up.

"Come, Father," Helena pleaded, helping him up.

Gerardo signaled the bus. Its brakes screeching, the bus halted a few yards beyond them. The conductor swung down from the step. "Is he coming?" he asked, nodding at the old man slowly shuffling toward the bus. "And that too?" He pointed at the wooden box.

"Yes," answered Claudio. He helped the conductor

stow the box in the luggage compartment at the back and followed his father inside.

"Hey, Claudio," Gerardo called after him. "Tell Father that María will be at the bus station. That is, if she's received the letter. María will help you when you arrive. She knows which bus you should take to go on down to. . . ."

But the bus started up, coughing as it accelerated, and drowned Gerardo's words. The conductor jumped like a cat onto the step, and they drove off in a cloud of dust.

Claudio pressed his face against the dirty window. He couldn't see Gerardo now, or Helena either. Gradually the familiar hills were fading into the distance behind them. "I can't see our house anymore," he said to his father.

The old man looked up. "Our house," he repeated. "Our house. . . ." His eyes gazed at the mountains in the distance. "Ah, those paths," he said, "I know them all by heart. I went to Ráquira over them with my boys."

"To Ráquira," repeated Claudio.

"Ah, that was before your time. Long before your time. You never went along then, but here we are going on a trip together after all. That's the way it is, Ave María." Still gazing through the window, he lapsed into silence. Now and then he thought he recognized a farm or a mountain peak. But the landscape changed rapidly until he did not know the hills anymore or the paths disappearing deep into the mountains. Everything was becoming strange, even hostile, to him.

When they arrived at the bus station in Bogotá, there was María in a blue suit with white blouse and white gloves. She seemed nervous and a bit impatient as she noticed her father and Claudio climbing down from the bus. She made as if to embrace her father, but she did not actually touch him. Turning to Claudio, she said, "You're late. I've been here for over an hour. We have to hurry, or you'll miss the other bus."

A real old schoolteacher, Claudio thought, as he followed her and his father through the crowd. There wasn't even time for a cup of coffee. When at last they reached the station, the bus was about to pull out. The motor already was throbbing.

"Get in, Father, quick," María said nervously.

"Yes, yes," mumbled the old man. "I. . . ."

"Come on up, my friend," called a young man from inside the bus. He bent down, grabbed Don Pacho under his arms, and hoisted him up onto the high step. Claudio, having put the wooden box once more in the back, climbed in also. When they had found a seat, he looked out. María was still there. She knocked against the window, nodded, and waved. As the bus drove off, she wiped her eyes with her handkerchief, and then waved again. The old man did not wave in return. Only Claudio raised his hand.

Leaving the city, the bus crossed the plains, and

then descended through the mountains. The road was steep and narrow, banked by deep ravines. The vegetation changed quickly. Even the cattle in the field were unfamiliar to Claudio.

It became steadily warmer. Don Pacho slowly struggled out of his coat and loosened his tie; he was not used to this heat. Then he bent down with difficulty and began fiddling with his shoelaces.

"What are you doing?" asked Claudio.

"Nothing."

"Can I help you?"

"Ah," said the old man, as he pulled off his yellow shoe slowly. He stared intently at his foot and then at the shoe in his hand. There was blood in it.

"What's the matter?" Claudio asked again.

"Blood."

"Blood! What from?"

"I don't know."

Claudio took the shoe, feeling inside it with his finger. "A nail," he said. "Quite a big one. Didn't you feel it when you were walking?"

"No." Don Pacho sighed and looked at the shoe with the blood in it. "They are the shoes I got married in. A pity. . . ."

"We can clean them. Later on, when we . . . when we arrive," said Claudio. "With a piece of paper or something."

"Do you want some paper?" asked the young man who had helped Don Pacho into the bus. "Here, take my newspaper. I'm finished with it." He handed his paper to Claudio.

"Would you like to read the front page?" Claudio asked his father. "We won't need all of it."

Don Pacho shook his head and looked out the window. The countryside was all strange: the coffee bushes under the shade trees, the banana plants, the small fields of sugarcane. There were no Holsteins to be seen anymore, only white zebu cows under the palm trees. He sighed again. Everything familiar to him he had left behind. The young man pulled out a bottle of *aguardiente*.

"Ave María, what a heat," he said. He drank thirstily and offered the bottle to Don Pacho. Don Pacho thanked him and drank in turn. He was hungry. They had not eaten since early morning, and in Bogotá there had not been time for even a cup of coffee! They drank from the bottle again.

"It's not like *chicha*," muttered Don Pacho disapprovingly. "*Chicha* is good when you're hungry or cold. . . ."

"Well, cold you won't be, for the time being," said the young man. "Virgen Santa, how hot it is. And it'll get worse. Where are you going?" He looked at Claudio, who was busy wiping the blood from the shoe with a wad of paper.

Don Pacho had taken off his other shoe and both socks. He touched the wound in his heel. It was deep and still bleeding, but he did not feel it.

"Where are you going?" the young man asked again.

"We're going to La Gloria," answered Don Pacho. "That's where."

"What?" asked the young man, bending forward and staring at Don Pacho. He couldn't believe he had heard correctly.

"To La Gloria de Santa María," repeated Don Pacho quietly. "That's where we're going. At home they told me that I'll get eleven pesos a day there. . . ."

"To La Gloria de Santa María?" The young man was shocked. "To the leprosy village, Virgen Santa!" He shrank away instinctively. Carefully wiping the rim of the bottle with the palm of his hand, he took another gulp of the fiery *aguardiente*.

3

The boy was lying at the edge of the ditch, almost hidden in the long grass. His attention was entirely concentrated on something he was watching there, his body tense as a hunter's. There was something in his hands.

Claudio couldn't see what it was, and he pushed the flowering shrubs a little further apart.

There were flowers everywhere. Never before had he seen a village with so many flowers as La Gloria de Santa María. At home, on the *finca*, they had only geraniums. But here hibiscus, bougainvillea, oleander, and poinsettias, all bloomed indiscriminately, their bright tropical colors mingled in a wild disorder. They grew around every house, even in the backyard of the neglected house where he now lived with his father.

The place belonged to Don Leonidas, and they helped him around the house and the garden, and did his errands. Luckily, Don Leonidas could not move around as he had no feet.

Don Leonidas also came from Boyacá. He had lived in the village of Ráquira. As he had been in La Gloria for more than thirty-eight years, however, Don Pacho knew Ráquira better than Don Leonidas did. Talking about Ráquira was what brought them together. When he heard that Don Pacho was familiar with Ráquira, Don Leonidas had taken them home immediately, and told them they could use one of the empty rooms for the time being.

So now Claudio did odd jobs for him and sometimes went on errands. For four evenings in a row his father had discussed Ráquira. Every evening the same conversation took place. Don Leonidas never grew tired of it. He followed them around in his wheelchair all over the house, through the huge bare rooms and out on the porch. "Tell me, Don Pacho," he would shout. "Come on, tell me."

And his father would begin the story all over again. Claudio doubted that his father could know much about Ráquira, since he had not been there for a long time. Already Don Pacho was describing events from their own village, using family names from Ráquira, of course. Claudio was shrewd enough to hold his tongue.

For several nights they had slept in the open air, not knowing where to go. Then they met Don Leonidas and found quarters in the big house. Claudio had been quick to perceive that Don Leonidas was a person of substance. His wheelchair was an expensive one, with

rubber tires, and it moved noiselessly. He had a heavy
cane with an ivory knob and a metal tip. If something
displeased him, Don Leonidas rapped it in anger on
the tiled floor. And if he swished it swiftly through the
air, a razor-sharp blade unsheathed from its metal tip.
Don Leonidas demonstrated the weapon to him the
first evening, and Claudio had been terrified when the
short, pointed knife suddenly whipped past his face.

"So that you know," Don Leonidas said with vi-
cious pleasure. "Nobody should think I can't de-
fend myself, though I'm confined to a wheelchair.
No, they certainly should not think that." He
sheathed its tip and carefully turned the ivory knob
between his broad, wiry hands.

And Don Leonidas certainly should not think
that I'm afraid of him, Claudio thought fiercely, as
he lay on his stomach among the shrubs. He edged
forward so that he was able to see the boy at the
other side of the ditch better. What could he be doing?

The boy was raising himself on his elbows now,
his eyes staring at the end of the ditch from which
a drainage pipe protruded. In the black hole of the
pipe something moved. A fat gray rat crept slowly
from the pipe, crawled around its rim, and then
held still. For a full second it stayed there motionless, its eyes in the pointed head darting back and
forth. Then it dropped cautiously from the pipe
and advanced along the ditch, its hairless tail leav-

ing a thin stripe in the dirt. The boy, waiting patiently, followed all its movements with the utmost attention.

The rat in the trench came nearer. Almost imperceptibly the boy raised himself a little, his eyes fixed on the animal. Then, closing one eye, he took aim with a slingshot. The rat fell, and at the same instant the boy dropped full length on top of it, his hands grabbing at it beneath its stomach.

"Got you," the boy said with the voice of a conqueror, as the rat set up a furious squeaking.

"Show me?" Claudio could not help himself.

"What?" The boy looked up, astonished.

"Show me," repeated Claudio.

The boy got up carefully, his hands still pressed to his belly. "Careful, you'll smother it," advised Claudio.

"Oh, it's not smothered that easily," answered the boy wisely. "But it wants to bite me, the wretch." He took the rat by the scruff of the neck and held it away from him.

"It's a big one," Claudio said in praise.

"So-so," answered the boy without enthusiasm. "Sometimes there are much bigger ones around. You've just settled here, haven't you?"

"Yes, with Don Leonidas."

"Where do you come from?"

"From Boyacá."

"We come from the coast."

"What's your name?"

"Alirio. What's yours?"

"Claudio."

One could tell that Alirio came from the coast, for his skin was smooth and dark, his hair tightly curled. The two boys looked down at the rat, which was struggling in Alirio's brown fingers. The thick gray body writhed, and the head turned to and fro. Its mouth was open, its sharp teeth plain to see. Claudio thought he heard it hiss like a cat. "What are you going to do with it?" he asked.

"I'm going to take it to someone who'll teach it tricks."

"Go on!"

"Really, it's true."

"To whom?"

"Ah. . . ." Alirio said, pausing mysteriously.

Claudio shrugged his shoulders and did not ask anything more.

Not getting the response he'd hoped for, Alirio volunteered, "If you go with me, you can see for yourself."

"Now?" asked Claudio.

Alirio nodded. "My mother doesn't want me in the house right now," he said. "She sent all of us outside." He glanced over at a house that was visible between the fruit trees and the flowers, its door and the windows tightly shut. In the yard several small children played under the supervision of an old sister. They all had the same frizzy hair, but the color of their skin varied from almost black to a golden brown.

"Are those your brothers and sisters?" Claudio wanted to know.

"There are fourteen of us," Alirio said with a shrug. "But Mother has sent all the older ones to the village."

"But why?"

"Because of Aura."

"Who is Aura?"

"My sister. She's the oldest. I come next. My mother says. . . ." Alirio didn't finish his sentence. The afternoon silence was broken by a sharp cry. In the house somebody had screamed.

Claudio was startled. "What's that?" he asked.

"Aura, I think." Alirio's smile was knowing.

At the same moment Don Leonidas appeared in his wheelchair on the back terrace of his house, his cane tapping angrily on the tile. "Claudio!" he shouted. "Claudio, where are you? What's all this screaming? Claudio!"

"Don Leonidas is calling me," Claudio said needlessly. He looked at Alirio and the rat. "A pity that I can't come along now."

Alirio shrugged. "Another time," he said indifferently. "I'll catch another one sometime. This one may be too old anyway. Still, I'll take it to Lucindo."

Claudio turned reluctantly in the direction of the house. He wanted to go to Lucindo's with Alirio. Suddenly he had an idea. "Listen," he said, looking back at Alirio. "If I find an errand to take me to the village, I can come with you after all."

"All right with me."

"Will you wait here for me?"

"Okay. That is, if you don't say anything about Aura," hissed Alirio with a look at the terrace, where Don Leonidas was impatiently wheeling back and forth in his chair.

"What?"

"Be careful not to say anything to Don Leonidas."

"Of course, not," answered Claudio. "I won't say anything." Quickly he ran home. He had no idea what he was to keep quiet about.

4

Claudio and Alirio walked together through the streets of the village. Even in the shade of the almond trees along the roadside it was hot.

Most people sat in the dark interior of their small house, their door open. Some were rocking in a cane chair, others lay in a hammock suspended across the room. Many of the faces were disfigured and expressionless, the inert bodies motionless. Some with bandaged legs and hands, or mere stumps of limbs, sat on the ground. A couple of men were throwing dice on a stoop. Two women whispered to each other as, half hidden behind a door, they peered out at the boys.

Claudio was carrying a sack of potatoes and a basket of corn and onions, while Alirio grasped the rat firmly between his brown fingers. As an added precaution, he had tied a piece of rope around the gray body in a kind of harness. He looked sideways at the basket swinging from Claudio's hand.

"You're lucky to live with Don Leonidas. I bet you have plenty to eat."

"Yes," answered Claudio, hoisting the heavy sack higher on his shoulder.

"Aura says the food is good there. She should know. She used to do the laundry for him, and the ironing as well. But now she doesn't want to go anymore."

"Oh, no? Why not?"

Alirio shrugged his shoulders. "Because she doesn't feel like it. He's a difficult old man, she says."

Claudio nodded understandingly. He had to admit that Don Leonidas was short-tempered and irritable, not one of the easiest people to live with.

"My mother says Aura is stupid," Alirio continued. "Don Leonidas is wealthy. She could be well off if she stayed with him. But now that Aura knows the young doctor she doesn't care about anything else. She's crazy, if you ask me. Here she is saddled with his. . . ."

"Yes," Claudio said. "That might be. . . ."

"Don Leonidas is old and rich. If she'd taken him, she'd be sitting pretty. At least, that's what my mother says! You can't tell, though. Maybe she'll change her mind."

"Mmm," muttered Claudio, thinking that if Aura came to Don Leonidas, they would have to leave to make room for her. What would they do then? he wondered. "Uh . . . what about that doctor?" he asked hesitantly.

Alirio's laugh was scornful. "Aura thinks that he'll marry her now. That remains to be seen. Look, there he is."

A car tore past them in a cloud of dust and stopped farther on in front of a large house. It was a delapidated building in a neglected garden tall with weeds.

"That's Doña Ana Eugenia's house," Alirio said. "She really is crazy, but not enough to be shut up in the asylum."

The boys watched the doctor get out of his car, walk up the path, and knock on the closed door. He was a thick-set man, with broad shoulders and a handsome face, and he had a well-groomed look about him. His hair shone with cream. On the hand that carried his doctor's case he wore a gold ring set with a blue stone.

"If we hurry, maybe we can look inside when the door opens," Alirio suggested. "We might see Doña Ana Eugenia then. She never comes out, but now . . . ." He strode along so fast that Claudio, burdened with basket and sack, had difficulty keeping up with him. They arrived opposite the house just as the door opened slightly.

"Yes?" a voice said through the crack.

"I'm here to see Doña Ana Eugenia," said the doctor, attempting to step inside.

The old woman behind the door did not budge. "Yes?" she asked again.

"I am Doctor Cárdenas. Alvaro Cárdenas. The *señora* sent for me," the doctor said.

The door opened a little more, but the old woman remained motionless. Coming to a halt on a level with the door, the boys tried to stare inside.

"Is that her?" asked Claudio.

Alirio shook his head. "No, that's Clorita, the maid. She's even older than Doña Ana Eugenia herself. She isn't sick, but she's just as crazy."

The woman in the doorframe blocked the doctor's way. She was old and grimy, her thin gray hair lying in disorder around her wrinkled face. "The *patrona* is not in," she said.

"Then where is she?" asked the doctor.

"She's working. She can't see anyone."

"But I'm the doctor," Doctor Cárdenas said, barely restraining the impatience in his voice. "Go and tell your mistress that Doctor Cárdenas is here. And hurry up. I have a lot to do today."

"*Ai, ai,*" complained the old woman. "The *patrona* is working. She's painting. She's quiet when she's busy with her pots of paint. Last night she cried, almost the whole night through. Now she's quiet again . . . ." The woman disappeared into the dark interior of the house, leaving the door ajar. The doctor did not wait. He pushed the door open with his case and followed the servant inside. The door slammed shut.

"You see," Alirio said with satisfaction. "Even the doctor had a hard time getting in. She never receives anyone, and she doesn't bother about anybody either. Like today. . . ."

"Does she really paint?" interrupted Claudio.

Alirio shrugged his shoulders. "You heard what Clorita says," he answered without interest.

"What does she paint?" Claudio insisted.

"Chicken feathers."

"What?"

"Chicken feathers," Alirio repeated.

"Chicken feathers? And what does she do with them?"

"She glues them together to make birds. All kinds of strange birds, like none you've ever seen, with wings of orange and purple and gold. My mother used to send me there with feathers from our big red parrot. She bought them and the green and yellow feathers from our parakeets too. Sometimes I shot a troupial in the hills with my slingshot and sold her the yellow and black feathers. That money I kept for myself. But later she didn't want the black feathers anymore, so I stopped. Besides Clorita told me that Doña Ana Eugenia's eyes are much worse, and she doesn't see well enough for such close work now. Sometimes the *patrona* busies herself painting the walls green. All dark green. . . . The woman is mad."

Claudio shifted the sack on his back and transferred the basket to his other hand. "Let's go," he said. They had been standing there long enough, he thought; they couldn't see anything anyway. The doctor was inside with Doña Ana Eugenia, who painted all the walls of her house dark green. The door remained tightly closed, and they walked on.

"Is it far to where you're going to take the rat?"

"No," answered Alirio. "We're almost there."

To Claudio, with his load, it still seemed a long way off. After all, Alirio had only his rat to carry.

"Here we are," Alirio said at last. Together they entered a small dark workshop.

Inside there was a workbench, on which lay a rusty vice, chisels, pliers, and files. In a corner was a pile of old iron and tin scraps, pieces of copper, and lead pipes. The workshop was empty, but in the small room behind they heard someone moving about. There seemed to be animals in there too.

Alirio went right on through, where it was even darker, to the yard behind. It was large and light, and to Claudio, who had followed hesitantly, it seemed filled with animals. There were chickens, rabbits, dogs, and two small black pigs. A turtle crawled on the ground, and a green parrot perched restlessly on the branch of a tree. In a corner of the yard a big wire cage enclosed many varieties of birds.

"*Mamacita, mamacita,*" the green parrot screamed.

"Yes, yes yes. . . ." said a man, busy stirring a pot set on a charcoal fire in the lean-to kitchen. "Hush, I'll be right with you."

"*Ola,* Lucindo," Alirio said.

The man looked up. He had a round, friendly face

with dreamy, light-colored eyes. "*Ola*, Alirio," he said in a soft musical voice. "Have you come to visit me?"

"Yes," Alirio answered.

"And who's that with you?" Lucindo looked at Claudio in a kindly way.

"Claudio."

"Ah, he's the one who lives with his father at Don Leonidas's house. You come from Ráquira, isn't that so?"

"No," answered Claudio.

"Oh, I thought you did. I thought you were relatives of Don Leonidas."

Claudio shook his head. "We have a *finca* on the other side of the *páramo*. But my father knows Ráquira well. Almost better than his own village."

"Ah," said Lucindo. "That's what I thought."

Suddenly something moved under his shirt, and a tiny, pointed head with fluffy ears appeared. A moment later a little woolly animal lay curled around his neck. It looked like a monkey.

"What's that?" Claudio asked.

"That's Tito," answered Lucindo, lovingly stroking the little animal. Claudio noticed his long, narrow hands. Tito walked a few times back and forth over the shoulders of his owner, and then disappeared again under the shirt.

"Look what I've got here!" Alirio held up the rat. "It's a big one, isn't it?"

"Yes, it's big."

"Could you tame it for me?"

"Who can tell?" Lucindo said frowning. "It's an old one, and they are not so easy to tame. It has its own ways already. Now if it were young, straight from the litter, it would learn more easily. These old ones are troublesome."

"Yes." Alirio hesitated, staring down at the big gray rat in his hands.

"Come and have a look," Lucindo said. He led the boys back inside the small dark room. In a corner stood a cage with delicate spokes and finely meshed wire. Inside an entire playground had been constructed, with a seesaw and tiny ladders and a kind of merry-go-round wheel. At the back was a house, looking almost like a church with its elegant little towers. The cage was full of mice. Lucindo took a straw from the floor and tapped it against the wheel. Immediately one of the mice jumped on a rung, and the wheel started to turn. Lucindo tapped on the seesaw, and another mouse climbed onto it. He laughed with pleasure. "You see?" he said.

"The mice are good," Alirio said, "but I thought . . . ."

"All right, look here," Lucindo said. Carefully he opened a tin can punched with holes, tilting it so that the light shone inside.

At first the boys didn't see anything. But then something moved between the green leaves at the bottom. A thick-bodied beetle with a metal shield attached to its back crawled slowly away from the leaves. Lucindo put his finger into the can, and the beetle crept along it onto the back of his hand. With a dirty nail he tapped on the copper shield.

"Isn't it beautiful?" he asked. "I made it myself."

"You made that?" Claudio could not believe his ears.

"Yes, but it was quite a job. Do you see those colored stones? I set them too. Now with the little chain and the clasp a girl can fasten it to her blouse. Look." He put the harnessed beetle on his shirt and fastened it. "You see, it can't escape."

"No, it can't escape," Claudio repeated, dazed.

Lucindo was looking at Alirio. "It's a brooch," he said. "It would be beautiful for Aura."

"Yes."

"I made it for her," said Lucindo.

"I see," Alirio answered.

"But she doesn't want it," Lucindo went on. "It's creepy, she says, although she didn't even see it. But she says she thinks a beetle on her blouse is creepy." His face darkened.

Alirio kept silent, and he began to poke at his rat.

"Why don't you tell her that you've seen it? That it's finished?"

Alirio nodded. "I'll tell her," he said casually.

Lucindo's face cleared. "She can also have the tin can. The tin can with the leaves. They must always be fresh."

"Yes, of course," Alirio answered impatiently. "What about my rat?"

"Give it to me. I'll see if I can do something with it." Lucindo first returned the beetle carefully to the can, and then took the rat from Alirio. He rummaged among the piles of junk, found a small cage, and put the rat inside.

"Maybe I can make a harness for it, and a small cart that it can pull as well." He glanced sideways at Alirio. "You'll tell Aura?"

"Yes, I'll tell her," Alirio promised. "When do you think it will be ready?" His mind was on his rat.

"Ah, that will take some time," Lucindo said. "You'd better come back and check. It's not as easy to tame an old animal as a young one, remember. I had one myself, but the dog killed it. And broke the cart too. A pity. . . ."

"Yes, a pity, a pity." A voice spoke from the room's dark corner.

Startled, the boys turned.

There on a heap of rags sat a very old woman, her hair in thin, gray wisps. Her legs, grown crooked, were wound with dirty rags. She scrambled nearer, using her hands. Through her grubby, flowered dress, open at the back, the boys could see swellings and sores on her skin. "A pity, a pity," she repeated hoarsely.

"Here are the mice, *mamacita*," Lucindo said, his voice gentle. "Come and look at the mice."

The old woman dragged herself up to the cage. Lucindo repeated the game with the straw. The mice obediently mounted the seesaw and made the wheel turn. Claudio couldn't tell if they were the same mice as before. The old woman pressed her face to the cage. Her toothless mouth smiled emptily.

"Nice, isn't it?" said Lucindo.

"Yes, nice, nice . . ." repeated the old woman in her hoarse voice. She continued to stare at the mice.

Claudio nudged Alirio. "Shall we go?" he asked. "I've got to get home." He went outside into the backyard to pick up his sack and his basket. Chickens were picking at the corncobs.

Lucindo went to the kitchen and began to stir the pot again. "*Mamacita, mamacita,*" the green parrot screamed.

"So you'll tell Aura," he reminded Alirio, as the boys took off.

"What?" Alirio had forgotten.

"About that beetle. Tell her I've finished the harness now, with the colored stones and the clasp. She might think about it. . . ."

"Oh, yes. I'll tell her," Alirio promised.

Outside he shrugged his shoulders. "As if Aura has nothing else to think about," he said mockingly. "Look, the doctor is off again!"

5

Florinda saw by the luminous hands of the alarm clock that it was half past nine. She was crazy to sit here in the dark this way. Just sitting and waiting. For what? For whom? Yesterday afternoon she had seen him go past, and he hadn't even looked. He just drove by, barely missing those boys.

"That wretch!" Florinda clenched her hands. They were white hands, but the revealing brown spots marred them. The spots were on her legs as well, and the skin of her forehead was rough and lumpy. She stroked it. Yes, there was no doubt. Shall I call? she thought. Shall I ask for new medicine? It was too late now. Tomorrow! She would call him tomorrow.

Suddenly she laughed aloud mockingly. She knew what was going on! Everybody had been able to see what had happened to Aura, hadn't they? Aura, that insolent stuck-up bitch, with her sound, healthy body. Her copper hair hung down to her shoulders, and her light skin was the color of liquid gold. She, Florinda, understood why she wore her hair as long as a lion's mane. Automatically she touched her own short, dry hair. It was getting thin already.

That half-grown boy, the dark one with the curls, was Aura's brother. Florinda had recognized him immediately. They all had their mother's stiff, frizzy hair, except Aura. She resembled her blond father, but had the almond-shaped eyes of her mother, the golden skin and the supple, catlike walk of a mulatto. Florinda scowled. Even during the last of the nine months Aura had been beautiful and supple.

Florinda got up, stiffly crossed the room to where she knew the mirror was hanging, and stood in front of it. But it was dark, and she didn't turn on the light. Why should she? She knew only too well what she would see. Besides, if she switched on the light the neighbors would notice. They noticed everything; they knew everything. Everybody in this damned village always knew everything.

As she felt her way to the little cupboard in the corner she bumped into a chair, and it squeaked on the tiled floor. In the back of the house a light came on, a door opened, and Nubia appeared looking out of her room.

"Did you call, Señorita Florinda?" She leaned against the doorjamb in her wrinkled nightdress.

"No, I did not call," Florinda said curtly. She was annoyed. "Go to bed!"

Nubia disappeared into her room, but she left the door ajar. Lying on her bed again, she listened intently. Yes, there was the door of the corner cupboard opening. Nubia grinned slyly.

Florinda felt for the bottle and one of the crystal glasses on the bottom shelf. She hesitated, remembering. Only a few months ago Alvaro sometimes dropped in during the evening, his doctor's case in hand. They had sat together on the wide terrace, looking out over the garden of which she was so proud. There were jasmine and salmon-colored hibiscus, and under the trees some rare orchids. Her house was spacious and cool, modern; its large windows on the street side were barred. It stood out from most of the houses in the village.

With Alvaro she had sat on the terrace in the dusk. They sipped at a drink and talked, about music and painting and literature. Sometimes they listened to classical music, or occasionally even danced to a record. But mostly they had talked, and those conversations had been islands of pleasure in the endless row of lonely evenings.

Once Alvaro had asked why she didn't visit Doña Ana Eugenia. A cultivated woman, he had said, not nearly as old as she seemed to be. And she was not feebleminded either, in spite of what people said. In fact, she was a very talented woman, a pity that she was so depressed. Florinda should try to make friends with her. Maybe she'd be able to cheer her up a bit.

If only she had done so, she would have an excuse now to visit Ana Eugenia regularly. Over there she might have seen him again. But at the time it didn't seem to make sense. Alvaro was coming to see her here. And why would she want to have anything to do with that gloomy shuttered house, with a person everyone said was queer and solitary, a person who never concerned herself with others?

Once more Florinda's groping hand found the bottle there among the writing paper, envelopes, a letter opener, pens, pencils, ink, and old correspondence, all put away together in disorder. Placing it on the floor, she felt for a glass, then hesitated. Should she take two glasses from the cupboard? Two? Maybe if she took two, he would come. Would she let him in, if he came this late? Everyone would know tomorrow. She took out two glasses, picked up the bottle, and returned to her seat at the window. Steadily she drank, one glass after the other. Soon she stopped waiting.

Inside the tightly locked house, smothered by the green enveloping wilderness of the garden, Clorita shuffled through the rooms. Yes, under her *patrona's* door, there was a sliver of light. Clorita fumbled at the knob. She knew that she could not help, but. . . .

"*Mi patrona,*" she called. "*Mi patrona.*" No answer. She remained there, listening. Maybe her *patrona* had gone to bed. Then she could go to sleep as well. Clorita shook her head. "*Mi patrona,*" she called again.

In the room Doña Ana Eugenia sat quite still, without moving, almost without breathing. She waited

motionless and silent, until she heard the footsteps
fade away in the echoing house. Relieved, she slowly
wiped the sweat from her forehead and dabbed at her
constantly running eyes, which were now so in-
flamed. With the shutters closed the room was like an
oven. The powerful lamp gave off heat, but little light.
The light was bad, so bad. Again she wiped her red-
dened eyes. She had little time left, she knew.

Now, while it was still possible, she must. . . . She
listened intently. Everything was quiet. Maybe
Clorita had gone to bed. She got up and tried to slip
softly, almost inaudibly, toward her bedroom, but not
softly enough. Again she could hear the shuffling footsteps of Clorita.

"*Mi patrona,* it's late. You should go to bed, *mi patrona.*" Clorita fumbled at the knob, then stooped and
held her ear against the door. In the room all was
quiet. Clorita bent forward, listening.

In the doorframe between the living room and the
bedroom, Doña Ana Eugenia stood stock still. She did
not feel the pain behind her eyes anymore, only a
sudden, flaring anger. Why didn't they let her be? The
endless vigilance, the creeping around, spying at her
through cracks and keyholes. Oh, she knew, she knew.
Like a child she was watched. Like a child! She would,
oh yes, she would. . . . She turned back into the living
room, going toward the corner with the pots of paint
and the brushes. Glancing around, she saw her paint-
ings of colored birds. The birds, composed of hun-

dreds of feathers, large and small, were bizarre, carefully arranged compositions. At last she took down from the wall a small golden bird and started to apply green paint with a thick brush. Hastily, steadily, fiercely she worked, until nothing remained of it but a thick green clot.

. . . as green as the hills around this wretched village, she thought. She did not remember that the sugarcane was ripening on the fields, that the hills and valleys around La Gloria were turning to yellow gold. Her thin, powerless arm continued its brush strokes, until the pain swelled again behind her eyeballs. Panting, she stopped. As she wiped her hot, washed-out face, she stared at her vanished golden bird.

"There," she said softly, her voice hoarse. "There!" Then she listened intently.

Behind the door stood Clorita. She also listened. They remained this way, each on one side of the door, for a long time.

Claudio sat with his father and Don Leonidas on the wide, tiled terrace behind the house. Don Leonidas was moving back and forth in his wheelchair. Back and forth, back and forth, his broad strong hands continually turned the wheels. Don Pacho, sitting at the edge of the terrace, was talking.

"It must be quite some years ago that I last saw Jaime Posada. Let me see, at least five or six years."

"When I left Ráquira, Don Jaime was an old man

already, with one foot in the grave. Don't tell me he's still alive?" grumbled Leonidas crossly.

"Or maybe it was his son," Don Pacho said quickly. "Yes, it must have been his son. His name was also Jaime."

"Ignacio," corrected Don Leonidas. "The son of Jaime was called Ignacio, although he was not a bit better than his father."

"No, he wasn't. Not a bit better," Don Pacho acquiesced hastily. He sighed.

Don Leonidas had the memory of an elephant. He remembered every detail from his past with exactness, and he wished to know in just as great detail how everyone had fared since he left. About his own family, however, he did not utter a word. Nor did he wish to hear about them either. For more than thirty-eight years he had not seen one of them. They never had come to visit him. Now and then a letter arrived, but he tore it up unread. He had not even reacted to the telegram about his wife's death.

"If they want to know whether I'm dead yet, let them come and see," he had said to himself with a certain satisfaction. "That's what they're waiting for! My money! But they'll wait for a long time yet. I'll outlive all of them, all of them!" He gave the wheels a hard thrust.

Don Pacho chattered away, desperately making up new stories to tell. Soon Don Leonidas interrupted, and addressed himself to Claudio. "Do you ever see the boy from the house behind here?"

"Yes," answered Claudio, reluctantly.

"Mmm, and his sister, do you know her as well?"

"No, I don't know her."

"Mmm," grumbled Don Leonidas. He peered at the house, barely visible between the trees, where Alirio and Aura lived.

When it was quite dark, a visitor arrived to see Don Leonidas. He was a tall, skinny man with a gray face and yellow, protruding teeth.

Just like Alirio's rat, Claudio thought.

"Pues," said the man. "I didn't know that you had visitors."

"I don't," Don Leonidas answered.

"Pues," the tall man said again, looking from Don Leonidas to Don Pacho and over to Claudio.

"They are members of the household," said Don Leonidas.

"Ah, so," said the man, sucking air in through his teeth.

Don Leonidas turned to Claudio. "Get the whiskey," he ordered, "and the glasses, mind you." He motioned to the visitor to sit down. "It's good you came," he said after a while. "The affair of Marta Mesa is unpleasant."

The stranger nodded, watching his glass attentively. "Did you lend her money?" he asked casually.

"Exactly. She was in rather desperate straits, poor

thing, deeply in debt, and then her husband died suddenly. The one on crutches, with one leg. He was ill, and it was his allowance after all, and the money stopped then. But she wanted to give him a proper funeral. That's understandable, isn't it? And the children, they have to eat. Yes, she needed money, poor thing. What else could I do but lend her some? With interest, of course. I'm not a philanthropist after all, and I'm not stupid either. People think that money grows on your back. Well, she returned a few times, always with a different story. You know how it is."

"Ah," said the tall, skinny man, waving his hand in acquiescence.

"The last time she came wailing here, she was all upset. She said that she had heard her dead husband walking at night. That's one for you, Don Fabio!"

The two men grinned at each other, and Don Leonidas refilled the glasses.

"She must have heard someone else walking," Don Fabio said. "In the dark all cats are gray."

"Who knows?" answered Don Leonidas. "She was sure her husband couldn't find peace, and so she was hearing the sound of his crutches. Well, that doesn't matter! The fact is, the money I lent her, with interest naturally, now comes to a considerable amount. But can she pay up? Oh, no! And that, of course, I can't allow."

"No," assented Don Fabio, sipping his whiskey. "That can't go on."

"Of course, she has that piece of property," Don Leonidas mused on. "It's a fairly good piece of land there, next to the river."

"Yes, it's good land," agreed Don Fabio.

"She pledged it as security."

"Yes, yes." Don Fabio barely concealed his impatience. They had had so many of these talks, and he knew the whole sequence by heart. Don Leonidas had his own way of coming to the point, and he never deviated from it. Still, everyone had his little peculiarities.

"Yes," Don Leonidas repeated. "Of course, it's hard on her. But you understand, my patience has reached its limit. If she doesn't pay this week, that property should be entered in my name. The sooner the better." He refilled the glasses again.

"So if you have a spare moment this week?" He looked at Don Fabio.

"Of course, I'll attend to it," Don Fabio answered, "whenever you let me know."

"I'll send the boy," Don Leonidas assured him, nodding in Claudio's direction.

"Splendid, splendid. I'll hear from you then," and Don Fabio departed into the darkness. All was silent.

A light shone suddenly on the back porch of Alirio's house. Alirio's parents, Benita de Fátima and Don Nepo, who sold lottery tickets in the village, came outside. They sat down in the patio under the naked electric light bulb, and the children of all colors from black to milky white crowded around them.

Claudio peered between the trees. Alirio was not there, nor was Aura. Don Leonidas tapped on the tiles with his heavy cane.

6

On the patio behind her house Benita de Fátima sat in her chair, the smaller children playing around her. In her broad lap she rocked the baby, who lay across the bunched pleats of her shapeless calico dress. She just sat there, dark and massive as mother earth herself, contentedly watching her numerous offspring. Humming softly as she rocked, she stroked the soft, round baby face with her fingers, their first joints missing.

It's a beautiful child, she thought with satisfaction. A handsome, healthy child, and a boy at that. She smiled. Well, she was lucky. All her children were beautiful and strong and healthy. Aura's child would be too. She glanced at the children playing in the garden. The big parrot screamed as Mauricio poked at it with a stick. The fighting cocks walked briskly to and fro in their cages. She had to admit that Nepo had beautiful cocks. The pig was beginning to fatten. She had a good husband in Nepo, one who took care of everything. Yes, indeed, of everything. Wincing, she moved her legs. The parrot deafened her with its sud-

den scream; the baby woke up and started to cry. She
tried to soothe it. The parrot still screamed, and the
pig grunted loudly in its corner of the garden.

"*Ai*, Mauricio, *mi amor!*" Benita de Fátima pleaded
with her son, who was poking at the bird. She lifted
up the baby in her disfigured hands and held it to her
heavy breasts.

"*Aruru,*" she sang softly. "*Aruru.*" The child kept on
crying. Maybe it's hungry, she thought. "Mauricio,
where's Aura? Go and call Aura."

"She's not here," Mauricio answered. "And Alirio
isn't either."

"Alirio not here? Where is he?"

"Gone. He and that boy from over there left early
this morning to cut sugarcane on Puerta Grande.
They took Father's machete, too. I saw it myself."

"And Aura, where did she go?"

Mauricio shrugged his shoulders. "How should I
know?" he answered.

Alirio away and Aura as well? Well, what could she,
Benita de Fátima, do about it? She rocked the baby
against her. The child, quiet now, lay staring up at
her. A sound, beautiful child, she thought again, as she
looked at the tiny face with its enormous eyes. Smiling, she began to sing.

"Is it far?" Claudio asked.

"No, we're almost there. Behind that hill is the big
house of Puerta Grande. You can't see it from here,

but that's where it is. We should try to find Nestor, the overseer. If we're lucky, he'll take us. They're always short of people at harvest time."

"Yes," Claudio said, not completely convinced. He mopped the sweat from his brow. It was already warm, and they had walked quite a distance up through the hills.

"Remember not to say where we come from. That's why I took a roundabout way through Palo Quemado. You mustn't tell them that we come from La Gloria de Santa María."

"Well. . . ." Claudio was doubtful.

Alirio vaulted the gate into an empty corral, Claudio hard on his heels, and together they entered the yard. Beyond, on a hilltop, was the stately white plantation house, surrounded by flower beds and fruit trees. Steps led to the wide, shaded veranda enclosing the house on three sides, and bougainvillea, in a riotous rainbow of colors, cascaded from the balustrades.

Alirio didn't even turn his head toward the house, but continued on between stables and barns, down a narrow path into the cane fields on the other side. "That's what I thought," he said, pointing. "Look, they've started work over there. Nestor will be there, I bet. Come on."

They followed the path between rows of tall cane, past groups of working men, all wearing kerchiefs under their hats to keep the sweat from their eyes. Brown, sinewy arms swung the machetes rhythmically, and the golden cane fell. Cutting off the narrow leaves, the men threw the stalks on a pile and worked on, row by row, across the cane fields.

In the distance a man rode on horseback, up and down among the men. "That's the overseer, that's Nestor. I told you we'd find him out here." But Alirio went no farther into the fields.

"Aren't you going to ask him?" Claudio was getting impatient. After their long walk, he didn't want to stand much longer in the hot sunshine. Perhaps it would be cooler among the cane stalks. When they started work, maybe he wouldn't be so thirsty. He wasn't used to this kind of heat, and he felt stifled.

"Okay, okay, I'll ask in a minute," Alirio answered. "When he comes this way again." Now that he was near his goal he was less sure of himself. Nestor didn't notice the two boys; he was shouting instructions at the men.

Suddenly two riders came galloping around a bend in the path. When they saw the overseer, they pulled up their mounts. "Nestor, how are things going here?"

Nestor touched his hat. "All right, so far, Don Manuel," he answered.

"Got any more workers?"

Nestor shook his head. "Not yet. It's busy all over now and hard to find people."

Don Manuel, the owner of Puerta Grande, loosened the reins of his horse. The animal stretched its slender neck. His rider relaxed in the saddle, hands on knees, and looked around. He spotted the boys immediately.

"And who are they?" he asked, pointing at them.

Nestor shrugged. "*Pues*, who knows?" he said.

Don Manuel beckoned.

As they drew near, Claudio could see that the other rider was a girl with a thin face and bluish-gray eyes. She had a slender waist and narrow hips; she wore faded jeans and a boy's shirt, which was darkened with sweat and pasted against her skin.

Her horse, a bay with a long mane and tail, was small and young and spirited. He turned his head from side to side, nostrils flaring. Apparently unaccustomed to the bit, he mouthed it impatiently and pawed the dust.

Claudio saw that the girl had difficulty controlling her horse. But she did not give in, and she did not seem afraid.

"What do you two want?" Don Manuel questioned them.

"We . . . we're looking for work," Alirio answered. His voice didn't sound as cocky as usual.

Don Manuel looked at his overseer, raising his eyebrows. "Here are two," he said.

Nestor nodded and looked the boys over. "Where do you come from?" he asked.

"We're together. We're looking for work," Alirio answered, one foot scraping the other leg.

"I see that. But where are you from?" repeated the overseer.

"From over there." Alirio pointed. "Farther on, behind Palo Quemado."

"I see." Nestor looked at his boss.

"You can take them as far as I'm concerned," responded Don Manuel, tightening his reins again and looking at his companion. "Come along, Pilar," he said, and galloped away.

Pilar was having a hard time controlling her horse. The nervous young animal danced sideways, chewing at the bit. Foam dripped from his jaws as he shook his head from side to side.

"Not so tense," Nestor advised, leaning toward the girl. "Keep control, but loosen the reins a bit." He slapped the bay on the haunch, and the horse shot away.

Alirio moved quickly to the side of the road, but Claudio stood his ground, filled with admiration for horse and rider. The bay missed him by an inch, and he could feel the sweating body as it went by. The girl's knee brushed his arm. Claudio watched as she galloped away, hair flying in the wind, hair as long as the horse's mane and the color of wild honey.

"Well, you heard him," said Nestor behind them. "You can start right away. Over there, with Miguel Angel, el Indio." Motioning with his hand, he turned his horse away.

Voices sounded on the path approaching the cane field, and two men appeared. Alirio nudged Claudio hard in the ribs. "They're from La Gloria. They're looking for work too! Quick, hide in the cane, and take care they don't see us."

They joined the nearest row of men and got busy wielding their machetes, keeping their heads down.

Nestor could be heard talking to the newcomers. "Not if you're from the village down there. No, I'm sorry. We don't have work for you."

"I'm healthy," one of the men said defiantly. His voice did not carry conviction.

"Maybe so," Nestor answered. "But Don Manuel doesn't employ anyone from down there. He won't have anything to do with the village, he says. *Pues*, can I help it?"

The men working among the rows of sugarcane raised their heads to peer between the stalks at the scene in the road. Miguel Angel, el Indio, an old man in rags with a flat monkey face, sucked in his lips over his toothless gums.

"Pah, they're from the village. Ave María. We won't take them, just as I thought. Now they're going."

"They look just like us," a workman remarked.

"Nestor saw through them, though." Miguel Angel, el Indio, spoke with obvious satisfaction.

The other looked at him sideways. "Well, you with

your shrunken head might come from there too," he said dryly. The others grinned.

"Ave María Purísima," said Miguel Angel, el Indio. Shocked, he made the sign of the cross. "If you only knew what walks around down there. Not that I've ever been there, of course. But my dead mother, God's mercy on her soul, often told me about it. Her neighbor's cousin worked there. It's a village of living corpses that haven't been buried."

"And it's overrun with children," another added.

"Only the children look normal. The rest are skeletons," Miguel Angel, el Indio, insisted.

"If you listen hard, you can hear them rattling like maracas," another field hand joked. The others laughed.

Michel Angel, el Indio, was not distracted. "The cousin of my mother's neighbor, may she rest in peace, worked at the cemetery there. And once a day he went through the village with a big basket and collected the dropped-off limbs." He looked at his companions. This time he'd silenced them.

Maybe what he said was true, they thought. Miguel Angel, el Indio, was very old—more than a hundred, if you believed what people said—and he knew much.

Nestor rode past, and the men turned back to their work. Alirio glanced sideways at Claudio. As the high stalks tumbled around them and they chopped off the leaves and the top, he said, "Don't forget to give me two pesos at the end of the week for renting the machete."

Claudio didn't hear him. He was thinking of the words of Miguel Angel, el Indio, and of Nestor's face as he rebuffed the men in search of work. At last he understood. Because he lived in the village, he, too, was marked.

7

Doña Paulina, Pilar's grandmother, sat on the cool, shaded veranda of the big house, watching the two men who were mowing the lawn with a critical eye. The grass should be short. Doña Paulina did not like finding snakes under her chair. From where she was sitting she had a magnificent view of the surrounding cane fields and the cotton and corn plantings farther down the valley. A small lake, bordered by tall, old trees, palms, and heavy undergrowth, lay as a dark patch between the slopes of hills beyond. The village was out of sight. Doña Paulina noticed Pilar coming across the lawn between the flowering plants and shrubs.

In a short yellow towel dress, with her long brown legs, the girl looked like one of the luminous yellow calyx flowers, which grew exuberantly between the big stones. The long honey-colored hair was dark and moist, combed smoothly away from her face. Waving at her grandmother with a wet towel, she stopped a moment to chat with one of the gardeners, who with a shy smile touched his sweaty hat. Then she climbed the veranda steps two at a time.

"Where have you been?" Doña Paulina asked, as Pilar dropped beside her.

"Swimming."

"Swimming?" Doña Paulina repeated. She hadn't heard a sound from the direction of the swimming pool. It must have escaped her. "I didn't know you were at the pool."

"I wasn't. I was at the lake," Pilar answered. She reached for the pitcher of fresh lime juice that stood, with glasses, on the table. Pouring herself a glass, she drank deeply.

"Warm," she said, making a face. "Isn't there anything else?" She turned toward the house, where Albertina was always to be found, never far from the sound of her mistress's voice. "Albertina!"

A woman as old as Doña Paulina came through the door. She was thin and bent, with a brown, wrinkled face.

"What do you wish, my heart?" she said to Pilar.

"Something cold. Very, very cold, with lots of ice. Do you hear?"

"You were at the lake?" Doña Paulina said, after Albertina had gone. "You didn't swim there, did you?"

"Yes, why not?" Pilar's voice was defiant.

"Because. . . ." Doña Paulina hesitated. The men on the estate adored Pilar, yet she didn't like to have her granddaughter go to the lake to swim. It was so far, so lonely. "You were alone?" she asked.

"Yes, of course. Who would I go with? With Nestor, do you think?" Pilar tried to pass off the question with a laugh.

But her grandmother was not amused. She frowned instead. With some disapproval in her voice, she said, "Why don't you swim here at the pool? Your father built it especially for you."

"I know." Pilar shrugged her shoulders impatiently. She didn't say anything more.

The pool was no fun, she thought resentfully. It lay in the full, glaring sun, because the trees around the basin had been chopped away. Its dainty blue tiles only made the water *look* cool. And always Albertina watched nearby, like a mother hen guarding her chicks.

But at the lake, in the shade of the trees, it was nice. She could sit for hours on a tree stump huddled in the green twilight, gazing about her. The purple glow of the water hyacinths on the dark surface, the flecks of light sifting through the trees, the stillness of the water, the mysterious, hardly audible lake sounds, a rustling behind the bushes, a bubble now and again breaking the surface. . . .

Was it true what Miguel Angel, el Indio, said? No, she had better not think of his stories.

Sometimes small fish swam past the tree stump. If she kept her feet utterly still in the water, they would veer toward them and come very close. Translucent, the fish were silver or sometimes red. Water birds dipped over the broad leaves of the water lilies, looking for insects. Dragonflies buzzed, and the round heads of tiny turtles broke the surface, only to disappear again. The lake was deep, at some places very deep. Was it true that long ago one of her family had drowned there, that she had been murdered by a servant?

"Sometimes she returns over the water, on the night of the year that it happened," Miguel Angel, el Indio, had said, nodding his withered monkey's face. "Or maybe on other nights as well. Who knows! She comes up all the way to the house."

Pilar hated the house! She hated its high, gloomy rooms with the fragile French furniture that did not fit. The huge gilt-framed mirrors, their old watery glass shimmering, were moisture spotted. Stern-faced family portraits hung on the walls, and on the grand piano, black like a coffin, stood the silver-framed portrait of her mother, always with a small vase of flowers in front of it. The house frightened her. Its silence was different from that at the lake. Somehow it seemed confined and dead. There were many rooms with locked doors, empty, shadowed rooms where no one entered. Or did they? They lived a very quiet life on the plantation. Nobody ever came to see them.

Her father and her grandmother talked no more than was necessary, and always coolly and impersonally. At the table her grandmother sometimes inquired after the state of affairs at the hacienda, and her father made a short report. But as a rule they were silent.

Her father's face was always somber; only when he looked at his daughter did he smile, a little absentmindedly. He would nod consent when Pilar asked him if she could come along to see the cattle or crops only to realize later he did not have the time. Nestor was sent along instead. Nevertheless, in his own clumsy way her father spoiled her, with the new swimming pool, with the young bay that he had bought for her, with the beautiful white calf he had given her.

They were not close, any of them; they had no real contact with each other. Her father lived for his work, often secluding himself in his study, where he slept as well. Her grandmother was old, strict, and silent, too. She ruled the household from behind the fine embroidery in her always busy hands. Pilar could not talk to her either. There was no one to talk to, except for Albertina, who shuffled through the house sighing and moaning and calling her "my heart."

Oh, she hated the silence of the old house. And at night, when even the motor that generated the electricity stopped, she was afraid. The floors of the locked rooms creaked in the dark, and sometimes she heard a stirring in the garden or a shuffling on the veranda. The tops of the old rain trees in the yard moaned in the breeze.

Many incidents she could not explain, not even in the clear light of day. The disappearance of a picture of her and Dagmé, the new bay; the withdrawn silence of her grandmother for days on end; the irritable outbursts of her father; their cool, almost hostile attitude toward each other. Sometimes they acted as if they could not bear each other's company, as if they would like to avoid each other altogether. All these things frightened her and made her feel insecure.

In her dreams, those recurring dreams, Pilar had the feeling that someone was watching her. Were they dreams?

Who was the woman who had drowned in the lake, murdered by one of her own servants? Why had she not found peace, as Miguel Angel, el Indio, claimed? Once Pilar had asked her grandmother about the story and promptly had been forbidden to sit in the yard or go to the mill again. But Pilar paid no heed. She liked the yard and talking to the men; she enjoyed riding over the hacienda, through the hills and cane fields, to the valley where the cattle were. The silent, dark lake, with its age-old trees, however, was what attracted her most of all. It drew her irresistibly.

"I prefer that you don't swim that far away," Doña Paulina said.

"Where?" Pilar asked, lost in her thoughts.

"At the lake. . . ."

Pilar did not answer, but looked annoyed. "Albertina!" she called.

Across the veranda Albertina came shuffling with fresh lime juice. Ice cubes tinkled in the pitcher. "Here, my heart," she said.

8

Aura walked through the dark streets of the village, not hurrying. She knew that the men on the steps of the houses looked at her. Paying no attention, she walked straight ahead, head held high, a little smile on her lips. She moved like a wild cat, soundless and supple, seemingly nonchalant, yet cautious.

Behind her she heard a car bumping along the bad road. Loose stones flew away from the impact of the tires. She was caught in the beam of the headlights, but she did not look around. Nor did she move out of the way. The car came on, then slowed up, Aura still in its lights. She continued looking straight ahead, even when the car drew alongside. She knew who the driver was.

"Aura," Doctor Cárdenas said softly.

Aura sauntered on, her pace long and graceful.

"Hey, *pssstt*, Aura."

Aura turned her head to look at him, her smile amused. "Good evening, Doctor," she said. But she did not stop, and the car kept rolling along beside her.

"How are you? How's everything?" he asked.

"All is well," Aura answered. Her eyes challenged him, and she did not slow down.

"Are you in such a hurry?"

"Not particularly."

"Where are you going?"

"Where could I go here in this village? Home, where else?"

"How are you?" the doctor asked again.

"Fine, everything's fine." Aura shrugged.

"Your mother has not come for medicine for quite a while."

"Ah, poor mother. She is busy, what with the children and the baby," Aura said.

"Ah, yes. Well, why don't you come? I can give the medicine to you."

"We'll see," Aura said. "My mother wants me to start work again."

"Yes?"

"With Don Leonidas. He's a good man, she says, and wealthy."

Doctor Cárdenas frowned. They had come to a straight, wide stretch of road, and he stopped the car, turned off the lights, and took out his cigarettes. He offered her one. Aura had come to a stop too, without being aware of doing so. He flicked on his cigarette lighter, and they looked at each other over the flame, their eyes clashing.

"Why don't you get in?" he said.

"I am almost home," Aura evaded, puffing the smoke deliberately in his face.

"We could drive around a bit. Then I'll take you there later."

"Yes, we could," Aura said, her voice teasing. She waited, and the silence was as taut as a drawn string. "But if Don Leonidas finds out, maybe he won't hire me," she finally answered.

"Don Leonidas can hardly move," Doctor Cárdenas said. "But it's true, in his wheelchair he's as agile as a weasel!" He stroked his dark, shining hair; then his manicured forefinger smoothed the thin mustache above his full upper lip.

"He has people with him now, relatives, I believe," Aura informed him. "The boy is all over the place. He might see me." She looked at him through half-closed lids, her body swaying slightly. The warm, sweet smell of her skin reached the doctor.

Impatiently he threw away his half-finished cigarette. It glowed in the grass at the roadside for a moment. "Maybe I could give you a job. . . ."

"Ah, yes." From the dark outside the car, Aura's voice mocked him. Then softly she challenged him. "Doing what?"

"As a doctor's assistant." The tip of his tongue flicked over his full lips, darting like a snake's tongue. They looked at each other, their eyes shining. The doctor opened the door, motioning with his head. He knew he had won.

"Come, get in," he said peremptorily. When Aura slid in next to him, he closed the door sharply, and for a moment she was held there, pinched between his arm and the plastic backrest.

Lucindo picked up the half-finished cigarette. It was still glowing, but when he puffed on the butt, it went out. He walked on, the dead cigarette in one hand and in the other the box with the ornamental beetle for Aura. Passing the window where Florinda sat, he hesitated a moment, then stopped.

"Good evening," he said softly in his sweet voice.

"Good evening, Lucindo," Florinda answered. "What's new? Anything?" She spoke rapidly, puffing nervously on her cigarette in its silver holder. One hand pushed her half-empty glass behind a vase filled with artificial flowers. "Anything new?" she repeated. "Have you been for a walk? Where did you go?"

"I'm coming from Aura's," Lucindo said.

"Oh, why?"

"She wasn't in," Lucindo said. He shook his head.

"Oh, no? Where was she?"

Lucindo hesitated. "Who knows?" he answered slowly. "Could you give me a light?"

Florinda's hand felt in the dark across the table. I hope I don't knock over the glass, she thought. She touched her lighter. "Here!" she said. She saw his face in the light of the flame. "Where did you get that American filter cigarette? Who gave it to you? Was it Doctor Cárdenas?" Her questions came rapidly.

"I found it," Lucindo answered, inhaling on the butt. The tip glowed like a firefly in the twilight. "I picked it up over there, along the empty stretch of road, when I came back from Aura's house." He gripped the box in his hand.

Florinda didn't ask anything more. She knew enough. She stared at Lucindo, and after a while she said, "What have you got there?" She was not interested.

"The beetle for Aura," Lucindo said softly. "She didn't come for it, so I was going to take it to her. I thought maybe Alirio forgot to tell her. But she wasn't there."

"What kind of beetle is it?"

"Look!" Carefully Lucindo opened the box. The beetle in its harness, its back set with colored stones, walked on his hand, and he held it up to her.

Florinda peered down. "Did you really make that? Why?"

"It's a brooch. See?" Lucindo attached the beetle to his clean shirt.

Florinda looked at the beetle in its shiny casing, but she was thinking all the time of Doctor Cárdenas's car on the dark road, not far from Aura's home. He had stood there. The cigarette was his brand. "Why didn't you wait until Aura came home?" she asked.

"No." Lucindo shook his head. "No, I couldn't wait. I can't leave my mother alone that long."

"How is your mother?"

"Ah, so-so. The same as always." He answered absentmindedly. "She sends greetings," he added in his pleasant voice.

"Give her mine," Florinda answered automatically. Her eyes wandered uneasily around the half-dark room. In the back of the house she heard someone moving. It was Nubia, of course, curious as always. She could picture the girl's plump, half-grown body, leaning against the doorjamb no doubt. She could feel the staring look of the eyes, with their sly curiosity. Florinda wished Lucindo would leave. She was thirsty. She wanted to be alone and think of Doctor Cárdenas's car; of how he had waited in the dark road; and of Aura, who had not been at home.

She had known about the baby for quite a while, the baby Aura's mother rocked in her lap. Everybody in the village knew all about it. Her eyes went from the chair at the other side of the table to the half-empty glass hidden behind the artificial flowers. Should she ask Lucindo to come in? No, she could not, with Nubia there in the dark, for tomorrow everyone would know. Alvaro also would find out, and then maybe he never would come again. There she went, still hoping for. . . . She looked at Lucindo again. He really had a nice face, a good one, very different from Alvaro's. Her eyes went to the beetle in its finely made harness and the colored stones. The beetle sat motion-less on his white shirt.

"Well, I'll be off," Lucindo said gently. Dropping the butt, he carefully put the beetle back in its box. "Be seeing you."

"So long," Florinda answered. When he had gone, she got up quickly and crept outside to where he had stood. Stooping, she picked up the cigarette butt. In-side once more, she shredded it with nervous fingers into the ashtray.

Across the road, a neighbor asked herself in aston-ishment what Florinda could have found in the dirt.

9

Until nightfall the melancholy sound of the sugar mill could be heard all over the valley. The wheels squeaked and creaked as the water foamed over the turning blades. Dark, sweet juice flowed from the golden cane as it slowly was ground into pulp.

Claudio no longer sweated in the cane fields. He now drove the donkeys, which plodded, heavily burdened with sugarcane, from the fields to the farm.

"*Harre, harre,*" he urged them on. It had been hot all day. Now it was getting cooler as the afternoon wore on. Claudio took a comb from his pocket and passed it through his wavy hair before entering the yard. He glanced in a little mirror that he had bought, at the same time as the comb, with his own money. He never had much left, for Don Pacho's eleven pesos a day still had not come through, and Claudio had to contribute to their board at Don Leonidas's. What's more, he had to pay Alirio for the rent of the machete.

It was busy at the mill. Men worked in the open shed, which loomed darkly against the steam wafting upward from the huge copper tubs. Women and children stood around and watched.

Claudio untied the twisted ropes with a jerk. The load of cane fell to the ground.

A man fed the stalks into the grinder in endless monotony. Greedy iron teeth seized them and pressed them into pulp. The juice flowed sluggishly through a wooden chute into the first container. Men ladled it from one copper tub to the next with long-handled buckets. In the dim light beneath the roof, clouds of wasps buzzed in the fumes filling the shed.

Miguel Angel, el Indio, tended to the fires beneath the tubs. His toothless mouth gaped contentedly. He liked to feed the flames, to listen to the dry compressed straw of the sugarcane crackle deep in the bowels of the flues beneath the row of copper tubs. The juice, hot and yellow, rose foaming almost over the smooth copper rims. The sweet-smelling steam whirled around as the liquid settled again. The buckets dipped into the glutinous mass as the syrup turned dark and thick. It was hot and humid, and the men were barely visible through the steam. Children nibbled at bits of brittle sugar they found among the straw on the concrete floor.

Once a child had fallen into one of the tubs. They had used the buckets to scoop him out, and the long handle of one of them had snapped under his weight. When they finally got him out, he lay on the concrete floor among the chaff like a solid syrup doll.

Alirio was busy washing the wooden lattice frames in which the liquid syrup would be poured to cool into brown cubes of *panela*. Wasps buzzed about him as he worked. The men stirred the syrup in the copper tubs. Miguel Angel, el Indio, pushed more chaff into the fire.

Claudio lingered near the mill, for he had caught a glimpse of Pilar among the crowd. She seemed almost ethereal, shimmering like spun sugar in the dark of the shed, with the wild-honey smell of the steaming juice all around her.

The syrup bubbled, changing from yellow to tan. It thickened and ran along the copper drains, from tub to tub, to the last one, where it remained simmering until the time came to ladle it into the wooden trays to cool.

Claudio watched Pilar as she bent to pull a stalk from the pile. Darting forward, she stuck it down into a corner of the tray. When the thickened juice covered it, she pulled it out and whirled it between her slender hands until the syrup solidified. She moved away and began to pull the sugar from the stalk in threads.

She was quite near to Claudio now, and he saw her throw away the sticky stalk and continue pulling at the brown-sugar threads, quickly folding them together again, over and over, until the tawny color changed to white, the white of the spun sugar called *melcocha*.

"Ah," said Miguel Angel, el Indio. "It will taste better with *aguardiente!* Look!"

He wiped his toothless mouth. Grinning, he produced a bottle of *aguardiente* from the heaps of chaff. "Hold out your hands. That's better," he said, as he poured *aguardiente* all over the *melcocha*. "*Melcocha* soaked in *aguardiente!* What more could you want?"

"But it's too much. Now everything stinks of it," Pilar said, wrinkling her nose in distaste. She looked at Claudio. "Do you want a piece?" she asked, holding out her hands.

He could not avoid taking some of the odd-shaped *melcocha*. Blushing, he muttered, "Thank you." Then, turning to his donkeys, he yelled at them to start them moving. He thought he heard Alirio giggling. Alirio didn't miss a thing, not Alirio!

"*Harre!* Get going!" he shouted at the donkeys, as he chased them on their way back to the fields.

Suddenly he became aware of footsteps following him. He looked around and saw Pilar.

"Hey!" she called out to him. Claudio stopped. "Do you work here now?"

"Yes."

"But you haven't been with us for long, have you?"

"No."

"Where are you from?"

"From, from Boyacá. My father has a *finca* there. A big one," he added.

"Really? Does he grow sugarcane and corn and cotton too?" Pilar asked. She had stopped also and was looking at him. Unconsciously Claudio flattened his hair.

"No, not sugarcane. Corn and potatoes; horses, too."

"Did you see my bay? He's a beauty, isn't he?"

"Yes, he is," Claudio assented. With a smile he added, "You haven't had him very long, have you?"

"How do you know that?" Pilar asked, raising her eyebrows.

"He isn't"—Claudio searched for the right word— "trained," he finished.

"He's still young," Pilar said. "Nestor rides him. But Nestor doesn't have much time."

"If you want, I can ride him for you," Claudio offered. He added with pride, "My father was the best horseman of the region."

Pilar pretended not to hear. "Where are your parents?" she asked.

"Oh, at home." Claudio was evasive. "My father's at home."

"And your mother?"

"My mother died."

"Mine too. My grandmother looks after me. She's very strict. She doesn't like it when I hang around in the yard and at the *trapiche*. You want some *melcocha?*"

Claudio hesitated. Dusk was falling. A light breeze stirred the sugarcane.

The *melcocha* had hardened in Pilar's hand. "Miguel

Angel, el Indio, poured too much *aguardiente* over it.
You can taste it, and smell it too. If my grandmother
knew!" She laughed and turned away. Without saying
good-bye, she ran back to the mill.

Claudio hastened after his donkeys, now plodding
far ahead of him. The last rays of sunshine gilded the
cane fields, still echoing with the sound of her silvery
laughter.

Claudio unloaded the animals and removed the sad-
dles. He waited for Alirio to finish too. The last batch
of *panela* was being carried to the barn. Alirio threw
the wooden strips from the frames into a trough of
water and wiped the table clean.

"That's it for today," he said.

"Yes."

"Let's go, Claudio. It's getting late."

"A dark night," a man said. "Maybe we'll have rain.
Listen to that wind. . . ."

"If it *is* the wind," Miguel Angel, el Indio, said
mysteriously.

"It is," the workman said again. "The rain is coming
now. Look at the lightning, there over the mountains."

They all turned toward the mountains, staring at
the dark sky in the distance and at the lightning flashes
that lighted up the night.

The wind swept over the cane-covered hills. "Ah,"
Miguel Angel, el Indio, said. "You can't convince me

that easily, brother. I've roamed these hills longer than you have."

"That may be," the other mumbled.

The men chuckled. Everyone knew why Miguel Angel, el Indio, used to go off alone. He'd take a narrow trail, through tall grass and thick shrubbery, past shaded palm groves and soggy paths along the lake, until he reached a solitary hut where a woman lived. Perhaps she was someone whose husband had run away, or perhaps she'd been widowed. But she was stuck there with a litter of children. The youngest was a mere baby, they said.

Miguel Angel, el Indio, chuckled too. His bleary eyes glowed. Well, he had quite a reputation! That could do no harm. He wiped his mouth with the back of his hand. "You have to have nerves of steel to pass the lake at night," he continued.

"Sometimes she's there, drifting in a rowboat. The same rowboat, it is, rotting, shining a fluorescent green. She makes for the shore; she wants to go back to the house, that's for sure. Sometimes the trees reject her. The branches hanging over the water slip away as she reaches for them. Then she drifts to the center again, to where it must have happened. There, where he pushed her over the edge of the boat into the water .... Ave María Santísima! My poor mother, bless her soul, witnessed his hanging, here on the hacienda."

"Here on the hacienda? Ave María!" a man repeated. Frightened, he looked over his shoulder. The men huddled together. The tall, old rain trees, their enormous branches covered with vines, like purple cataracts, creaked in the wind. Heavy branches reached out. Those very branches perhaps. . . . Who could tell!

In the shadow under the trees donkeys and mules stood in a tangle, rubbing restlessly against each other. In the dark they merged into a single animal. It looked like *la mula de tres patas,* the devil himself, in the shape of a mule with three legs. Ave María! At night in the dark, with the shadows, the whispering silence, one never knew what could happen.

"I saw her once, when the moon was bright," Miguel Angel, el Indio, said pensively. "Ave María, I'll never forget it. I don't scare easily. Nobody can say that." He looked around. No one spoke.

"It was on a Sunday night. I'd been to mass, and we had drunk some at a tavern in Palo Quemado. It was getting late, so I thought I'd take the shortcut, past the lake to Puerta Grande. It was harvesttime, just like now, and there was plenty of work the next day. We toil from the cradle to the grave, and what for! So when I noticed her, I thought she was one of the young women from around here. A pity to miss out on anything that comes my way, I thought, and I quickened my pace. *Pues,* yes! Then I still got hot at the sight of a moving skirt!"

Miguel Angel, el Indio, wiped his mouth again and continued. "She was dressed in black, and she kept in

front of me on the path. In the moonlight I could see
her clearly; she had a mantilla covering her head. She
was swift as she glided through the moonlight. I could
hear her skirts rustling around her hips, like the wind
through the sugarcane. I hissed at her between my
teeth, I had them then, but she didn't hear me, or
pretended not to, because she didn't look around. The
bitch, I thought. I was so near then that I could smell
her. A strange smell, Virgen Santa, that should have
warned me. But no! I hissed again, and she slowed
down, her mantilla blown by the wind, the long skirt
fluttering around her. Then suddenly she stopped and
slowly turned around.

"Ave María, she had no face! Behind the mantilla,
the eye sockets were filled with water, the hand holding its lace folds was transparent as glass, the bones
alone were visible. And that smell, the way the lake
can smell! My skin prickled all over, even my scalp,
and my teeth rattled in my mouth. Yes, they shook
loose that night, all of them. That's why I remember
so well. . . ." He fell silent, folding his lips around his
gums. His head shrank between his hunched shoulders, as if he wanted to hide.

The storm was nearing. Thunder and lightning
rolled through the hills. As a blue flash lighted up the
sky, it illumined the tired faces of the men, and Pilar's
drawn features too. She stood motionless, close to the
mill, listening and watching intently. Claudio noticed
her slightly parted lips and her enormous eyes that

glowed with excitement, expectation, and barely concealed fear.

The face of Miguel Angel, el Indio, seemed flatter
than ever, wrinkled and older too. "When I feel the
skin of my scalp prickle, when I catch that smell in the
wind, then I know that she's around. Somewhere she's
gliding in the shade of the shrubs or on the path along
the sugarcane. I know that she's come from the lake.
Maybe she's waiting for me," he added softly. "Maybe
she has come to fetch me. . . ."

10

The tall, skinny man, Don Fabio, had come again, and Don Leonidas was tapping his heavy cane angrily on the tiles of the back porch. Claudio had found out that Don Fabio was a judge, with much influence in the village. He was feared more than he was esteemed, but he was a friend of Don Leonidas's. Claudio was aware that Don Leonidas was influential too, treated by everyone with great respect and civility. A person never knew when he might need him, because Don Leonidas was always ready to help in business matters; he was even prepared sometimes to lend money. He could be generous too, if he felt so inclined.

"In my opinion, you'll be satisfied, Don Leonidas," Don Fabio was saying again. "It's a good piece of land, there by the river, and the registration in your name didn't take long."

"Yes," Leonidas mused. "Yes. . . . I still feel it's a pity, though, that there's another piece of land between it and the one I own already. It would be good if all three strips were joined. Easier to work! More profitable as well. As it is now, with that piece of land in between. . . ." Angrily he hammered the floor again with his cane. "I don't even know who owns it," he added with annoyance.

"That can be found out, of course," Don Fabio said with a grin.

"Yes, of course. But even then. . . . Well, we'll see. The property would be more valuable, naturally, if it were joined together. More efficient to work and easier to supervise. . . ."

Don Fabio interrupted him, keeping his voice low. "Of course, you could put *him* in Marta Mesa's house." He looked toward Don Pacho, pottering around at the hen house in the semidarkness. The old man was spending most of his time now caring for the chickens, and he even had managed to train a young pullet to follow him around.

"Mmm," Don Leonidas was not convinced. Clearly he did not appreciate suggestions from others. "Pacho isn't a bad type at all. He does all kinds of odd jobs, and he talks. He amuses me with his stories, and I like to have him around. But old Pacho is quite sick. More ill than I am, that's for sure!" Don Leonidas barely subdued his satisfaction at this thought.

"And his boy?" Don Fabio asked.

"Ah, Claudio. He has a job."

"Yes, where?" Don Fabio's voice was casual.

"Over at Puerta Grande."

"Really! He works there, does he?"

"He's a capable boy, that Claudio," Don Leonidas said. "I really appreciate someone who puts his shoulder to the wheel, and he pays his board here as well. Don Pacho hasn't received any allowance yet. He's on the list, of course, but others will have to die off before his turn comes to get the eleven pesos, and that may take some time."

"Maybe something can be arranged, so that he's put at the head of the list," Don Fabio suggested. "Sometimes influence is an asset. Maybe I could speak to one of the doctors."

"Doctors!" Don Leonidas repeated, snorting with contempt. "All those doctors can do is. . . ."

Abruptly he stopped. A swarm of children, wearing paper hats and carrying noisemakers, ran into Benita de Fátima's garden. Don Nepo and Aura followed and began to hang Chinese lanterns of different colors among the trees. Benita de Fátima shuffled over to her rocking chair. Seated, she watched them all contentedly. She held a bag of sweetmeats, and as she rocked the baby in her broad lap, she popped a candy into her mouth every now and then.

The children blew their noisemakers, and the big red parrot started to walk uneasily up and down on its perch, clapping its wings and shrieking piercingly. Unperturbed, Benita de Fátima surveyed the scene, sometimes giving a piece of advice to one, or uttering an admonitory word to another.

"*Ai*, Mauricio. Careful, *mi amor*. Alirio, go and help

your father with the lanterns. He's tired, poor thing."

"Yes, yes, I'm tired," admitted Don Nepo. Throughout the hot day he had been selling his lottery tickets in the streets. Now he went to sit beside his wife.

"They are beautiful children," Benita de Fátima said with undisguised pride, looking at her offspring. "Beautiful and healthy too! Fourteen, there are. Fifteen with the baby!"

"Yes, fifteen with the baby," Don Nepo repeated with a sigh.

Benita de Fátima patted the baby's healthy skin with her withered fingers. White as *melcocha*, he was, with hair as soft as silk! Carefully she wiped saliva from the corners of his mouth.

"The noise is driving me crazy," grumbled Don Leonidas. "Another feast day, of course. Those people from the coast do nothing but celebrate, and they shouldn't even be in this neighborhood. They have their own section in the village. They. . . ." He did not finish his sentence.

All the lanterns were alight now. In the center of the gay brightness was Aura. She had taken the baby from her mother and was rocking him gently.

"Aura! Aura!" her brothers and sisters called as they crowded around her. They jumped up and down, they patted the baby, and they tooted on their noisemakers. The baby began to scream.

"You and your noise," Aura said. "You frighten him, don't you see?" She was in the middle of the circle, and the glow of the lanterns played over her golden skin.

"Aura, sing for us?"

"Me? Sing?"

"Yes, yes, Aura. Sing a song for us!"

The girl's laughter, so clear and gay, carried to the ears of Don Leonidas and Don Fabio, watching from the back porch of the other house.

Don Pacho, who had hobbled back from the hen house, heard her too, and Claudio, who was carrying whiskey for the men on the porch.

Don Leonidas moved his chair restlessly. "That piece of fallow land," he mused. "I'd like to have that . . . ." But his gaze was on the lighted-up garden, his eyes focused on Aura.

"Come on, some music for your mother," Benita de Fátima called out. "Alirio, go get the tiple and your father's guitar and your drum and the maracas. Mauricio, *mi amor*, give them a hand!"

Alirio and Mauricio disappeared into the house, returning with the instruments. The children crowded around their parents like a swarm of bees. Soon the soft strumming of the guitar and the tiple was heard, then the staccato rattle of the maracas. Under Alirio's strong brown fingers the dull beat of the drum became louder and louder.

Now the singers joined in. "In the soft, dark evenings, on the beach by the sea. . . ." Aura moved and swayed to the rhythm of the tune, her strong, young voice leading them. The unsteady quaver of the smaller children was accompanied by guitar, drum, and maracas. The husky voice of the mother was filled with melancholy and longing.

"Never again shall I see that dark, golden beach by the sea," Benita de Fátima sang. "White, foamy crests . . . ." The waves came rushing through the hills, breaking and vanishing in the mountain ranges. Tear-stained stars fell among the blades of grass and died like fireflies.

On the veranda of the other house the men sat in silence, listening to the song of the sea. They stared at Aura, dancing in the light of the lanterns, with the child in her arms.

The song ended. The final strains of the melody played by the instruments were drowned in the sudden blare of a car horn. Aura, still carrying the baby, slipped into the house. Don Leonidas began his perpetual rapping on the tiles and ordered Claudio to fill the glasses. His voice was angry.

Pouring the whiskey, Claudio asked himself why he had thought of Pilar as he looked at Aura.

Benita de Fátima started another song.

Doctor Cárdenas sat at the wheel of his car, driving slowly past the house. He wondered, annoyed, why on earth he had honked his horn. For a fraction of a second he had caught a glimpse of Aura with the child. He had enough worries as it was! He drove down the dark lane and into the driveway of the doctors' house, where he and four other doctors lived. Each weekend one remained in the village, while the others went home to their families. The house was thick-walled, spacious and cool. Each doctor had his own apartment, and each led his own life. They saw each other in the clinics, at mealtimes, and occasionally had a drink together at the swimming pool at the far end of the overgrown garden. However, they did not make a practice of visiting with each other.

When Doctor Cárdenas pushed open the door and went into his one dark room, he felt he was not alone. "Hello?" he said aloud.

No answer. Quickly he felt for the light switch on the wall. There on one of his gay, chintz-covered chairs sat Florinda, blinking in the sudden light.

"You," Doctor Cárdenas said, annoyed. Pulling himself together, he added, "An unexpected visit." He took out a pack of cigarettes and offered her one, waiting patiently until she had managed with her clumsy fingers to put it in her holder. Then he gave her a light and stood there watching her.

"I . . . I was frightened tonight," Florinda said. She smiled diffidently.

"Frightened? What of?"

"I don't know. Sometimes everything hurts. This morning I wanted to come during your consulting hour, but I was afraid to in the heat. I was dizzy and short of breath. I thought this evening. . . ." She began to talk faster. "Sometimes the walls seem to close in on me, and there's a deafening silence in my ears. Sometimes I feel I can't stand it any longer in this damned village. You, you can go home every once in a while, to your relatives and friends. But I. . . ."

"If you want to, you can go back to your family for a visit." Doctor Cárdenas tried to speak reassuringly. "I've told you so before. There's no reason why not, you know."

"They don't want me at home," Florinda said, listlessly. "Oh, they don't say so to me. But I know just the same. When I'm home, my brothers and sisters can't have their friends in. And . . . and. . . ."

"What a stupid prejudice," Doctor Cárdenas said impatiently. He began to pace the floor. "If you like, I'll write a note to your parents, or I could call them and explain. I could tell them that you should have a bit of a change."

Dismissing the suggestion, Florinda shook her head. "There's nobody to talk to," she whispered. "Nobody. Every day is the same. Yesterday, tomorrow, today . . . . Please, give me another cigarette." Her voice became hoarse, more vague.

"I'll find something to help you sleep tonight, and I'll take you home," said Doctor Cárdenas, turning toward a cabinet in the wall.

Florinda spoke to his back. "You promised me a record, do you remember? A while ago."

"A record?" He was puzzled.

"Yes, you said I should hear it. Bach, I believe."

"Oh, that. Yes, indeed. Wait, I'll find it for you. Here, put these in your pocket." He handed her some tablets and went to the record rack.

"There's no hurry," Florinda said hastily, getting up. "You can find it some other day, when you have time."

Doctor Cárdenas followed her to the door. "I'll take you home," he said without enthusiasm, preceding her to the car. It was dark outside. The crickets chirped; the fireflies flared and disappeared again in the tall grass and among the bushes. A night bird called. The house lay alone in the overgrown garden, surrounded by the utter blackness of open country.

"Don't you lock your door?" Florinda asked in the car.

"The door? Oh, my door. No, I usually forget."

"You really should remember. One never knows," Florinda said. Her tone was anxious.

Doctor Cárdenas did not answer, vexed at her meddling. He could look after himself.

They drove through the village's narrow, bumpy streets. The night was sticky, the air full of dust. A faint, sickly smell hung among the houses. There was always that sickening smell, especially when it had not rained for a while. He thought bitterly that he, like Florinda, was fed up with the village and its sick people. Completely fed up. Again he thought of starting his own practice, in town, far from here, but he needed money for that. Abstractedly he stopped in front of Florinda's house. He opened the door of the car, but did not wait for her to open her front door. Florinda watched the red taillights disappearing around the corner of the street. She stood there. The empty hole of the door seemed more ominous than ever, and the walls came sliding toward her.

Why did I go? she thought. Why? He had clearly rejected her. He had taken away an illusion. She did not have many left. He had humiliated her. Yes, that's what he had done. Moving awkwardly she crossed the empty center of the room and bumped into the corner cupboard. By accident, she reassured herself. Opening its door, she reached for the bottle, there among the writing paper and the old envelopes. For a moment her hand closed around the narrow brass letter opener. Taking out bottle and glass, she groped her way to the bamboo seat on the terrace.

The doctor's car glided through the deserted streets of the village, on past the tightly shuttered house of Doña Ana Eugenia. There was something in that house, almost smothered in its encroaching garden, that had caught his attention when he'd been there last. What was it? In his thoughts he retraced his last visit and saw Doña Ana Eugenia, thin and shapeless in her dowdy dress. The long sleeves hid the dark, revealing blotches. He could see her still face with its washed-out features, and the lackluster streaming eyes. He thought of her rebellious moods, her explosions of anger followed by long periods of inertia, and that wrinkled old servant shuffling through the house, watching her *patrona* like a faithful dog, and for a mere pittance probably. Obviously though, Doña Ana Eugenia was comfortably off. She never lacked expensive medicines or good food either.

Doctor Cárdenas smiled. Not much remained a secret in this village. That big house. What was inside it that had caught his attention? Her strange-looking birds, fabricated out of thousands of tiny colored feathers? Fantastic, unreal, but still quite well done. The pots and tubes of paint, the pencils and the brushes? The dark green walls? The smell of turpentine and paint that could not smother the pervasive smell of the sick person? That unkempt old woman, Clorita, who looked after her? Perhaps now and then she dusted the furniture with a dirty rag, without moving the ornaments, or straightened the old books. What was it that he had seen?

Suddenly he knew!

He drove around the block again, past Doña Ana Eugenia's house once more. He took in the front, hardly visible among the vines, the hermetically locked shutters. He would pay her another visit, though it would not be easy. Clorita opened the door only an inch to callers, and Doña Ana Eugenia never received anyone. But he was her doctor. He would succeed. Doctor Cárdenas smiled. His foot pressed the accelerator, and he drove homeward.

11

Pilar sat on a tree stump that leaned, almost horizontally, over the lake. With her arms around her legs she gazed into the muddy water below. Its dark mirror reflected her face, her shining hair, the red of her bathing suit. She wanted to immerse herself in the water, for it was unbearably hot even in the deep shadow under the trees. But she lacked the courage. Once or twice she stretched out her leg and dipped her foot in. The water of the lake felt cool on her skin. If she kept her foot still long enough, hundreds of small fish came to the surface, whirling around its whiteness. And then, if she moved her toes, they suddenly vanished down into the depths.

Could the tales of Miquel Angel, el Indio, be true? The boat on the water that looked fluorescent green in the moonlight? The pale figure trying to reach the bank and the house where she, Pilar, now lived? She looked at the far shore. The palm trees were motionless, their dark crowns straight and proud in the blue haze of the sky. The age-old trees at the edge spread their branches far over the water. Would they really move back out of reach, if a person tried to grasp them? And who was she, that woman? A former owner of Puerta Grande? One of her forebears? She was supposed to be young and beautiful, Pilar recalled. Miquel Angel, el Indio, must have said so, because her father and her grandmother never mentioned the subject.

Maybe, Pilar thought, maybe it hadn't happened long ago. Maybe the woman was not one of her great grandmothers. But then who?

Behind her a twig cracked and branches snapped. Pilar sprang up. Motionlessly she stood on the tree stump. Who could it be? Nobody ever came to the lake.

The bushes parted, and Claudio pushed through, leading Pilar's bay by a length of rein. The other part of the rein trailed on the ground by the horse's hooves.

"How come?" Pilar asked, sounding stern and at the same time surprised. She looked at the broken rein and frowned.

"He must have got loose," Claudio answered, coming to a stop at the shore between the tall grass and fragrant wildflowers. Pilar remained on the stump. She looked like a brilliant flowering vine on the gnarled, old wood.

"He got loose and then . . . ?" she asked imperiously.

Claudio smiled, his teeth white against brown skin, his eyes glowing. "He came to the plantation," he said, "and I noticed him. At first I thought he had thrown you off, but when I saw the broken rein I realized he must have been tied up and torn loose."

"Thrown me off!" Pilar repeated. For a moment she seemed to be angered. Then she threw back her head and laughed. "And how did you know I was here?" she asked Claudio.

"One of the gardeners told me that you come here sometimes. So I . . . then I thought. . . ." Confused, Claudio fell silent. "It's quite a walk for you back to the plantation," he finished.

"You're right, and in this heat."

"Exactly, in this heat."

"But how did you manage to find this exact spot where I always come?" As Claudio smiled again Pilar decided that he had a nice face. When he was serious, it seemed remote, inscrutable.

"Because once I knew where to look, it was easy to find the track. I just followed it."

The bay was getting restless, stretching his slender neck. Claudio took him to the water's edge, removing the bit and slipping one end of the rein around the horse's neck. As the horse drank, Claudio dropped down on the stump beside Pilar. She was sitting again, dangling her feet in the water. The air quivered, hot, still, and heavy.

The bay waded farther into the lake, and they watched the widening circles on the surface. In the ripples their reflections merged.

"If I keep my foot still," said Pilar, "lots of fish come around it. Millions of fish, all silvery and transparent."

"Guppies, I think," Claudio said.

"Yes, maybe so."

"They're not there now, though," he said.

"No, they're not."

"Is it deep here?" Claudio asked.

"In some places it's very deep."

"This is the lake . . . the lake where . . . ?"

"Yes, at least that's what Miquel Angel, el Indio, says."

"Do you think everything that old man says is true?" Claudio asked hesitantly. He remembered hearing about the gravedigger with his big basket going through the village to pick up the dropped-off limbs. The village was his, and he knew the story was a flagrant lie.

"Yes, no, I don't know," Pilar answered. She looked frightened, as frightened as on the evening when Claudio had seen her at the *trapiche*. She sat motionless, and he watched her without speaking. The silence swelled and hovered over the dark water, quivering among the slanting shadows of the trees.

"Sometimes, sometimes I think he's right," Pilar said softly, almost inaudibly. "But. . . ."

"But?" Claudio repeated, hardly daring to breath.

"But sometimes I think that it's not quite the way he tells it. Not so long ago, for instance."

"You mean that woman in the boat?"

"Yes."

"Why do you think so?"

"I don't know. Just. . . ." Pilar looked around at him quickly. No, he wasn't laughing; his face didn't look forbidding. He seemed to be listening intently. Reassured, she went on. "Do you ever have the feeling that someone who doesn't exist is near you?" she asked.

Claudio did not answer immediately, but thought about her question. "No," he said at last.

"I do!"

"How do you mean?"

"I don't know. I can't explain it."

"You mean someone who has died?"

"Yes, or was murdered. I don't know which. Someone who hasn't found peace and returns. Maybe she wants to take possession of the house again, of her room." Pilar suddenly shivered. "She comes there," she added in a whisper. "I feel it. . . ."

"Maybe you dream it."

"Well, maybe, but. . . ." She hesitated, then continued. "It's a dream that keeps coming back. Time and again I have the same dream. I know someone is watching me. I can't see anything, but I feel it. . . ."

"And then?"

"Once I woke up and my grandmother was standing by the bed. She held a candle in her hand and she looked at me. I had the feeling that she wasn't alone, and yet there was no one else in the room."

"In the village," Claudio said, "in Boyacá," he

amended hastily. He faltered for a moment. How could he be that stupid!

Pilar was watching him, her eyes large. "Yes?" she asked.

"In our village in Boyacá there's a woman who says she hears her husband walking around the house at night."

"She hears him? How does she know it's him?"

"Because. . . ." Again Claudio hesitated, wishing he had not started on this subject. "He had had an accident, and he walked with a crutch. She heard his crutch."

"Oh," Pilar whispered. She looked frightened once more.

"Of course, it's all a lot of nonsense," Claudio said, his voice harsh, almost matter-of-fact. "If that woman only thought for a bit, she would have realized right away that he couldn't walk on his crutch. He never would have been buried with his crutch."

"Ah no, of course not!" Pilar sighed in relief. "Of course not," she repeated.

"So it's not true," Claudio said firmly.

"No, and yet. . . ." She could not get rid of the feeling that sometimes someone was there in the big house, on the veranda, somewhere. . . .

"It's an old wives' tale like that one Miquel Angel, el Indio, tells about. . . ." Claudio faltered again. No, he shouldn't say anything about that man with his basket. He must not talk about the village. If he said too much he and Alirio would lose their jobs at the hacienda, and Alirio would murder him. That was certain. He wouldn't see Pilar anymore either. That was certain, too.

The bay backed out of the water, then turned to wade along the shore. He splashed, and small pearly drops of water leaped into the air. Pilar and Claudio got up at the same time and stood on the tree stump facing each other. Pilar looked like a dewy, red flower. Claudio was suddenly very much aware of her. If she slipped, if she fell, she would hold on to him. Pilar was suddenly conscious of her wet clinging bathing suit. She blushed, feeling uncomfortable, and looked at her clothes, far away on a stone on the lakeshore.

"I must go," she said hastily, suddenly embarrassed. Then, in her usual tone of voice, she commanded, "Come on, hurry up."

Claudio jumped from the tree stump, still holding the horse by the broken rein.

"You can tie him for me farther on," Pilar ordered.

Without answering her, Claudio disappeared from sight. When he had gone, Pilar jerked the yellow dress over her head, on top of her bathing suit. She rolled the rest of her clothing in a bundle in her towel, thrust her wet feet into her shoes, and tried to run a comb through the wet tangle of her hair. Impatiently she shook it back as if she wanted to shake herself free of all the unspoken words, of all her mixed feelings and bewildering thoughts, and leave them forever in the enclosed blackness of the lake, in the depths of its dark green water.

Unnecessarily noisy, Pilar strode through the bushes, head high, a cold smile on her lips. She found the bay, his reins tied to a tree, but Claudio was nowhere to be seen. Undoing them, Pilar noticed that the broken ends of the reins had been fastened together with a thin strand of wire.

She would ask Nestor to mend the break properly for her.

12

When Claudio and Alirio entered, Lucindo was in his workshop, filing a piece of copper.

"What's that?" they asked.

"A lizard."

"What?"

"I'm making a lizard. Look." He laid aside the sharp, thin file and showed them his work. "It's not ready yet," he added, as though excusing himself. Claudio and Alirio looked on in silence. They could see it wasn't finished, and yet the copper already had the shape of a lizard, a head with tiny eyes, the large mouth, the long, narrowing tail.

"It's not finished yet," Lucindo said again. "The skin has to be hammered, and the tail has to be fixed a bit. And then I have to find stones for the eyes. That won't be easy. Red stones, or maybe green, I think."

"Why are you making it?" Alirio was curious.

"No reason," Lucindo answered with a shy smile. "Just for fun."

"Are you going to sell it?"

"Sell it? No, I don't think so. That didn't enter my mind," answered Lucindo. "I just wanted to make it."

"There's a woman here who knots handbags out of maguey, and a traveling salesman takes them and sells them in town. Without saying they come from here, of course." Alirio added with a sly grin.

"Well?" Lucindo said, doubtfully.

"I could sell it to that man for you." Alirio glanced sideways at Lucindo and pointed at the copper lizard.

"Well," Lucindo repeated. His tapered fingers stroked the metal back lovingly. "I'm not sure I want to sell it. . . ."

Alirio shrugged his shoulders. "What nonsense," he said. "Why are you making it then? The money would be worth your while."

Lucindo did not answer.

A woman entered the shop. "Ah, Lucindo," she said.

"Good afternoon," Lucindo greeted her. "How are you? What's new?"

"Nothing much. How is your mother?"

"So-so," Lucindo answered. "So-so." Then more softly he added, "The same as always."

"Ah, poor thing," the woman said with compassion, shaking her head. Then she continued in a business-like tone of voice. "I came to ask when you mean to come and mend that pipe. It's still leaking."

"The pipe? Ah yes, the pipe! That's true. I'd completely forgotten about it," Lucindo said, looking guilty. "I'll come as soon as I can manage. Tomorrow perhaps."

The woman pressed her lips together to show her displeasure. After a moment's silence, she said, "My husband can't do it himself. That's the way it is, if one doesn't have hands to work with anymore." She shrugged her shoulders in discouragement, then looked at Lucindo and the copper lizard in his hands. "What's that?" she asked.

"A lizard," Lucindo answered. "But it's not finished yet."

"What's it for?"

"Nothing special. For beauty, perhaps for fun," Lucindo answered shyly.

The woman shook her head in disapproval. "For fun! For beauty! As if you can live by that. You'd do better to keep your workshop running. Then you'd earn some money. Who'll buy that, I want to know!"

"But I don't want to sell it," Lucindo answered.

The woman shrugged once more. "At Doña Ana Eugenia's things seem to be upset again," she said, changing the subject. "Quite upset, the man in the drugstore told me. Clorita was there at an early hour to get tranquilizers. Doña Ana Eugenia has started painting everything green again. Now it's the furniture. At first all the walls, and now all the furniture. Can you imagine! Afterward she sits down and cries and cries and cries, for hours on end. The whole house smells of paint, because Doña Ana Eugenia wants it closed tight. In this heat! She should be locked up for a while, if you ask me! I can't understand why the doctor doesn't do something. Doctor Cárdenas, I mean." When she mentioned the name of the doctor, she watched Lucindo attentively, but he was silent, his face expressionless. The boys held their breath waiting for what would follow. But she said no more and left the workshop.

Over her shoulder she called, "You'll come tomorrow, Lucindo?"

"Yes, yes, tomorrow. Tomorrow, I'll come," Lucindo assured her, without looking up from his lizard.

"How about my rat?" Alirio asked.

"Ah, your rat!" Lucindo's face cleared. "I call it Napoleon," he said. "Come and look." He preceded the boys through the dark room, where a heap of rags in the corner moved and rustled.

"Eh," a hoarse voice said. "Who is it?"

"It's the boys, *mamacita*," Lucindo said. "They've come to look at Napoleon." Followed by Alirio and Claudio, he went into the backyard where birds chirped in the big cage. Pigs, chickens, dogs, rabbits, and turtles wandered around. The green parrot clung with its sharp nails to a dead branch. "*Mamacitaa, mamacitaaa,*" it shrieked, raising its head from its breast.

"Yes, yes," Lucindo said placatingly. "I'll take you to *mamacita* soon. Look, there's Napoleon," he said to the boys. "I built him a large, sturdy cage, as you can see, to keep him safe, because Tito is very jealous. See, what did I tell you?" He pushed Tito down the neck of his shirt. "Keep quiet, you," he said repovingly to the monkey.

The heavy gray rat sat in a corner of its cage, looking at the visitors with fierce little eyes.

When Lucindo slid his fingers over the wire, it raised itself on its hind legs. "You see?" Lucindo said proudly. "At first he wouldn't have anything to do with me, but now he knows me."

Alirio was not impressed. "Does it know tricks already, like the mice?" he asked.

"No, not yet. Everything takes time, after all. I'm busy now making it a little cart with metal wheels. And then it will get a harness. But that will take some time."

"Oh." Alirio was disappointed.

"Did you tell Aura about the beetle?" Lucindo asked after some hesitation.

"About the beetle?" Alirio asked, puzzled. Then he remembered his promise. "Of course," he said with conviction. "I told her immediately."

"What did she say?"

"Aura says she's afraid of beetles."

"Did you tell her about the copper harness I made, just like gold?"

"Yes, I did, but she still thinks it's creepy. Can I help

it?" He shrugged his shoulders. "Maybe she'd like to have the lizard," he added slyly.

"But I made the harness especially for her. As a brooch, you see, with all those colored stones." Lucindo sighed.

"*Mamacita, mamacitaaa,*" shrieked the green parrot furiously. Lucindo went toward it in his own deliberate way. Once more, among his animals, his expression became contented again.

Don Pacho would like it here, Claudio thought. His father could handle animals well too, though in a different way from Lucindo. There were many kinds here while Don Leonidas had only chickens.

Lucindo, the parrot on his shoulder, the boys following, went inside to the corner where the old woman sat on the floor. Seeing the boys, she tried, with skinny hands, to smooth her skirt down over what remained of her legs. They smiled at her, embarrassed.

Lucindo put the parrot next to her on the floor. She watched his every movement, and a slight smile appeared on the emaciated face with its blunted features and infected eyes. The parrot jumped onto her lap, and then began to walk up the skinny arm, claws hooked around the shriveled skin.

"Careful," Claudio warned. "It will hurt her."

"She doesn't feel it anymore," Lucindo said. "Isn't that right, *mamacita?* You don't feel it anymore?"

The old woman did not answer, and the parrot went up and down her arm. "*Mamacitaa,*" it shrieked.

Just like my father, Claudio thought. He didn't feel that nail in his shoe.

"Coming?" Alirio asked, sauntering toward the workshop. Claudio followed.

Behind them they heard Lucindo say, "Do you want to swing, *mamacita?* Shall I put you in the hammock?" As Claudio looked back over his shoulder he saw that Lucindo, with tender care, was lifting his mother into the hammock. He touched it gently, and *mamacita* rocked slowly to and fro, to and fro. . . .

When they were out in the street, Alirio said, "Shall we walk past it?"

"Past what?"

"Past Doña Ana Eugenia's house."

"Why?"

"Just to have a look."

Claudio shrugged his shoulders. "All right," he said without enthusiasm. They strolled along, stopping in front of Doña Ana Eugenia's. There was nothing to see. The doors and windows were tightly shut. Dusk had fallen, and the first purple shadows of the coming night clung to the shrubs and vines.

"Do you see anything?" Claudio asked.

"Ssst!" Alirio pricked up his ears.

"What?"

"Ssst!"

"But what?" Claudio asked impatiently.

"Don't you hear? She's crying. You can hear her."

They kept silent now, listening intently. From the closed house a soft moaning could be heard; it was plaintive, as though a child were crying and could not stop.

Alirio opened the gate without a sound, sneaked through the front garden, and glided over to the little archway at the side. Claudio followed cautiously.

The entrance to the inner court was locked, but Alirio dug a knife from his pocket and slipped it between the door and the doorpost. The lock opened without a sound. They pushed the door open and stood inside on a narrow path overgrown with weeds. Vines climbed against the side wall of the house and partly covered the large shuttered windows. The weeping was clearly audible now. Taking turns, the boys tried to peer through the shutters, but they could not see a thing. It was dark inside, and the slanting slats of the shutters kept them from making anything out. A door opening inside startled them, and they stood rooted to the ground.

"*Mi patrona*," an old voice whispered.

There was no answer.

"*Ai, mi patrona*, say something. Here, I have some fruit juice for you. You should not be naughty."

The weeping stopped.

"Here, drink this. It's cool," the old voice persuaded.

Alirio nudged Claudio. His mouth formed the word "Clorita." Claudio nodded in understanding.

"It's dark here," said the hoarse voice of Doña Ana Eugenia. "Dark and hot."

"Yes, it's hot. Clorita will open the windows a bit," the old maid said.

"No," Doña Ana Eugenia commanded.

"But, *mi patrona*, it's cool outside now."

"What day is it?"

"Sunday. Shall I ask the doctor tomorrow to come and see you again?"

"I don't want to see that doctor again. He takes my things away, you hear? Everything. He thinks that I don't notice it. . . ." The voice faded. Doña Ana Eugenia started to cry again.

"Shall I ask Father Andreas to come tonight?"

"No, no, I don't want to see anyone, not you either. Go away."

"*Pues,*" said the old maid. "*Pues.*" She lingered.

"Can't you leave me alone!" Doña Ana Eugenia shouted hoarsely. "I want to be alone, alone! Go away. Do you hear me? Go!"

Clorita went and Doña Ana Eugenia started to cry again, with long drawn-out wails.

Claudio nudged Alirio. He made a movement toward the street with his head. Alirio nodded, and the two of them sneaked through the archway and pulled the door shut softly behind them.

"A pity," Alirio said. "A pity that we couldn't see anything."

"Yes," Claudio assented. "Do you think those birds that you told me about are in that room?"

Alirio shrugged. "Maybe," he said indifferently. "But if she's painting everything green again, she'll mess around with all those colored birds until they're as green as Lucindo's parrot. Well, that's her business."

"Yes," Claudio answered absentmindedly, his thoughts with Lucindo and the little work of art he had made. "That lizard is going to be beautiful," he said.

"What?"

"That lizard of Lucindo's is a beauty. Just like the real thing. Its long sharp tail is like a dagger."

"Lucindo is stupid. He could make a lot of money if he'd sell those things. I know someone, and I can arrange it easily."

Claudio started laughing. "When Lucindo takes you as his go-between, there won't be much left for him," he jeered.

"Oh, come on." Alirio was offended. "Business is business, you know. And everything Lucindo would get, would be a gain for him, true? They live on the eleven pesos a day his mother gets. When she pops off, Lucindo will have nothing at all, because he doesn't work. And he thinks that my sister. . . ." Alirio laughed scornfully.

Claudio didn't answer. The thought occurred to him that when Lucindo's mother was dead and buried, his father would have a chance of getting his allowance. It was about time. Claudio was more than fed up with Don Leonidas. What's more he did not trust Don Fabio, who was always dropping in.

13

Pilar sat on the low wall of the veranda, looking out over the hills. Sugarcane stood everywhere, golden yellow with purple tassels. The noise of the sugar mill droned monotonously in the twilight. It was getting dark, and the valleys were filled with shadows. But Pilar was hardly aware of anything. She gazed pensively into the distance, her eyes seeing nothing. Nor did she know what she was thinking about. Her thoughts were unclear and undefined, vague and confusing.

Albertina came shuffling along the veranda. "Well, my heart," she said, "what are you doing, sitting here all by yourself? It's almost dark."

"Let me be," said Pilar.

"It's getting cool. I'll fetch your ruana."

"I'm not cold."

Albertina picked up the red swimming suit, which lay in a wet heap on the balustrade. "I'll hang it up to dry," she said. Pilar said nothing. She sat very still, her arms around her knees, her favorite position.

This afternoon Pilar had sat the same way on her tree stump, and then she had gone into the water. Right across the lake and back. She swam again and again until exhausted. She had decided not to let herself be upset anymore by the tales of Miguel Angel, el Indio. Later on she sat on the tree stump, waiting. Suddenly Pilar realized she was waiting for something. Dangling her feet in the water, she watched the translucent little fish darting up only to disappear again.

Guppies, Claudio had called them. Of course, she had known that too. But he had been thoughtful to bring her horse back. Another farmhand would have done so only if ordered to. Obviously Claudio was not an ordinary worker. His father had a hacienda too. In Boyacá had he said? Curious, that he'd be here, working for her father. Perhaps he wanted to learn about other crops, for they did not grow sugarcane where he came from. It was good to know a little bit about everything, and her father was pleased with him. "An intelligent boy," he had remarked to Nestor, and Nestor had agreed.

"Quick to catch on and a steady worker," he had added.

And a good hand with a horse, Pilar thought, remembering the afteroon when he had led the bay back to her by the lake and they had sat together on the stump. Admittedly she was staying at the lake longer than usual, hoping that Claudio would come.

Of course, she knew that he could not come. He was working in the cane fields and at the yard. Once or twice she had caught sight of him, and she was almost sure that he had seen her too, though he gave no sign.

She would have liked to have him come again and sit next to her on the tree stump. Just as before. Then they could have talked together. Claudio was sensible, serious too. And he was strong, with broad shoulders. He was not afraid of things, the way she was. Maybe she imagined so many things, because she was left alone so much, because she had nobody to talk to. Especially at night, when the lightning seemed to accentuate the silence, she felt abandoned. Then the past broke away from the shadowy corners on fluttering wings, and fear crept through the dark rooms. Then the old house was alone with its secret.

Was it true, after all, what they said? Or was it all imagination? What about the strained, tense relationship between her father and her grandmother, almost as if they hated each other? Was that her imagination also? She did not know, and she could not ask anyone, not even Claudio. Or could she? He might reassure her and tell her that the idea was nonsense. Last time their conversation had helped.

Far away in the valley she heard the long drawn out "*Oi, oi,*" of the hands as they drove the cattle before them. She had not gone there to look at her calf for a long time, she realized. But now Nestor was too busy, and her father did not like her to go that far alone. She would ask him if Claudio could go with her.

Albertina shuffled toward her. "Are you still there, my heart?"

"Yes," Pilar answered.

"But it's almost dark, and it's chilly now."

"I'm not cold," protested Pilar. But she shivered.

"You don't want to get sick, Pilar. Besides Doña Paulina is asking for you, and you have to change for dinner."

"Is my father home yet?"

"No, but any moment now, my heart."

Pilar stood up, unhurrying, and followed by Albertina went to her room. It was large, with high ceilings, thick white walls, and tall windows. Albertina turned on the light. Immediately brown moths plastered themselves against the screen.

"You must take a bath, my heart. You smell all muddy." Albertina stopped and looked at Pilar. "You didn't go to the lake again, did you?" she asked.

"Yes," Pilar answered defiantly.

Disappearing into the bathroom, Albertina turned on the shower and came back. Shaking her head, she said, "Why do you go there? You know Doña Paulina doesn't want you to. Why do you do it then?"

"I don't know," Pilar answered with less assurance than before. She could hear the water splashing in the shower. "It's so beautiful there."

"The lake is dangerous," Albertina said. "It's deep and full of waterplants and clinging weeds and. . . ."

Pilar raised her head. "Yes," she said. "Yes, I know."

"And there are water snails."

"I never saw them."

"No?" Albertina mumbled. "Perhaps not. But there are other things one never sees, Ave María Santísima."

Pilar stared at her. But Albertina was taking clean clothing from the cupboard. Pilar could not see her face. "What is it that one cannot see?" she asked. "Tell me !"

"Ah, my heart, so much, so much," Albertina said, sighing.

"Then it *is* there." Pilar spoke loudly, emphatically. "That's what I feel: something I can't see, but is there. What is it? What is it?"

Albertina turned around, startled. The expression on her old, wrinkled face was one of fear. "Child, what are you talking about?" she said. "Don't say such things. You are too young. . . ."

"What has that got to do with it?" Pilar said rebelliously. "I know it. I feel it."

"Here is your blue striped dress," Albertina said abruptly, putting it on the bed. "You like to wear this one."

Pilar did not say anything more. She stared at the dress on the bed, not really seeing it. For a moment they were both quiet. Only the splashing water in the shower broke the silence in the room.

"Have you everything now, my heart?" Albertina said. "Soap and towels and. . . ." She was about to leave the room.

"Albertina?"

"Yes, my heart."

"You must sleep in my room tonight."

"What? What's that?"

"Just as before," Pilar said. "I want you to sleep in my room again!"

"But. . . ."

"The night frightens me," Pilar said in a small voice. "Sometimes I believe. . . . I don't know what I believe. That woman who was murdered on the lake . . . . Who was she?"

"*Pues*, my heart, how should I know? It was so long ago. Someone of the family, I believe. . . ."

"Was it my mother?" Pilar asked.

"Your mother? Ave María Purísima! God bless her soul," Albertina whispered. "My child, how could you think. . . ." She left the room quickly, silent as a shadow, as if she fled from something.

Pilar sat motionless on the bed. The shower kept on running. Huge dark moths fluttered against the screening and hung there motionless, like hollow night eyes gazing at her. Pilar covered her face with her hands.

14

Claudio woke with a start, bathed in sweat. It was stifling hot and pitch dark. The whole house was permeated with the cloying smell of the sick old men. He could hear his father stirring in the bed against the other wall.

He stayed in bed for a while, turning restlessly this way and that, listening to the old man's rattling breath. Then he sat up and swung his legs to the floor. He groped in the dark for his shirt and pants at the end of the bed and put them on. Careful to make no noise, he crept out of the room. It was less dark outside, and he could make out the trees, dark and crooked, their branches reaching high into the air.

The house was utterly silent, and no sound came from Alirio's either. Claudio wondered what time it was. He crossed the porch and walked around the house to the street. The village was deserted. House doors were closed. In the half light of the starry night the place seemed somehow insecure in its emptiness. Heat from the day now past lay heavy between the houses, and the scent of flowers mingled with the sickly odor that characterized the village. With no rain, even the nights were hot and oppressive.

Claudio strolled through the empty streets, which had the appearance of dry, eroded riverbeds. Beyond the village the air improved. The path that Claudio followed was narrow and only faintly defined. Soon it disappeared altogether among tall grass and shrubs. White zebu cows stood under slender palm trees. Cicadas rasped, and the night quivered with their shrill, monotonous sound. Ahead of him Claudio could just make out the large black patch that marked the tall, old trees surrounding the lake. He could not see the water, but he knew the lake was there, smooth and shining in the light of a thousand stars.

The story that Miguel Angel, el Indio, had told about that woman who was murdered there. . . . Had she known what was coming, had she put up a fight? Who was she? How long ago had it happened? Tonight Claudio went out of his way to avoid the lake. Of course, whatever Miguel Angel, el Indio, claimed was all a lie, most of it anyway. That gravedigger with his basket was rubbish. Limbs did not drop off. They slowly rotted away, yes, but that was something else. There were plenty of people without fingers, without toes, with amputated legs and stumps of arms. He could see them sitting in an open door, on a canvas chair, or simply on the concrete floor of a dark hut, their bodies inert as if death had taken them already.

Their eyes looked out, but did not see, did not follow a figure as it came past. Sometimes the sound of a radio blared from inside the huts, but the inhabitants did not seem to hear it. He, Claudio, was still conscious of the sickness, but Alirio had become used to it.

Claudio was thinking of asking Alirio if Aura could use her influence with Doctor Cárdenas, to get the allowance of eleven pesos a day for his father. Then maybe they could go and live on their own in a room somewhere and not stay with Don Leonidas any longer. But Alirio was a sly one. He did nothing without pay. He made money out of everything, rent for the machete, which his father did not even miss, for instance. He even had tried to sell Claudio the rat that Lucindo was training. Alirio must have thought he was crazy. What use was a rat to him! As soon as he had saved enough money, he would buy his own machete, the biggest one he could find, and he could grind it razor-sharp!

Without knowing how he had got there, Claudio suddenly saw the dark outline of the sprawling mansion looming on the hill ahead of him—Puerta Grande. He stopped short and looked around.

There was no light anywhere. Slowly he went on. He was aware that he walked very cautiously, keeping in the shadows of trees and bushes. He was near the house now, facing the high veranda with its stone steps and its cascades of flowers. It seemed long past midnight, and even the cicadas had stopped their wailing. It was very still, a deathly stillness, as if every-thing—he himself, the old house, all of nature—was waiting.

Claudio held his breath, his body tense, motionless, his eyes riveted on the house, listening, waiting. Nothing happened, and gradually he relaxed. By chance he was at Pilar's house, and his eyes searched the dark, yawning windows curiously. Which of them was hers?

In the yard a dog started to bark. As he watched a shadow emerged from the back stairs and disappeared almost immediately into the blackness under the rain trees.

Claudio stood frozen. Had his eyes deceived him? No, he had seen a dark form slipping soundlessly across the terrace and down the back steps into the night. Still the dog whined. Somewhere a door opened. He heard voices. Somebody snapped at the dog.

As quick as lightning Claudio ducked down between the shrubs. What if Don Manuel or Nestor were to find him here! He crawled backward without a sound, his eyes fixed on the house. Was someone coming? Treacherous shadows, patches of light and dark, quivered among the trees. But nobody came and the voices fell silent.

Like a shot he turned and ran, through the garden and down the hill. The footpath! Without thinking, he took the shortcut, the narrow winding path that went past the lake.

And suddenly he saw her! For a moment he thought she was Pilar. He ran even faster and was about to call, "Pilar!"

But Claudio halted just in time, for the figure was not Pilar! The woman in front of him was different. She was older and dressed entirely in black. He stumbled on a stone, and it rolled down the path. He wanted to hide, but it was too late.

The woman stopped. Very slowly she turned. O God, behind the mantilla she did not have a face, and the eye sockets were hollow dark pools.

Claudio stood rooted to the ground. Miguel Angel, el Indio . . . the woman . . . the lake . . . went through his mind. So the story was true! He wanted to run, but he could not move.

Again the woman turned slowly and slipped away in the uncertain light of the stars, merging into the shadows as though erased from the earth. The spreading branches of the trees guarded the lake from view.

15

At the parish house, Father Andreas was sitting alone in his cell-like room. It contained a bed under a mosquito netting, a desk, two chairs, that was all. A crucifix hung above the head of the bed. Over the desk there was a picture of the Virgen de Guadalupe in her blue gown studded with stars, against a background of dark red, the color of roses he once had picked in the mountains of Mexico.

Mexico, Father Andreas thought, gazing at the Virgin Mother. Almost without thinking, he opened the top drawer of the desk, and his trembling hand took out a thin, finger-stained booklet. It was filled with brightly colored pictures of Mexico, its wide streets, tall buildings, vivid market scenes, the illumined cathedral on the large square, and those flower-laden barges on the wide canals between floating gardens. This small village with the canals and the multitude of colors had been his birthplace. Sometimes it had been warm there, yes, but not like this suffocating heat that hung among these hills. Ah, Mexico. . . .

Father Andreas shook his aged head. He had been away for a long time, and he never would see it again. For many years he had been here. Ah, he was old!

A knock came at the door, and when a rosy-faced young father looked in shyly, Father Andreas was startled. He pushed the booklet with its colorful pictures quickly into the drawer.

"Father Andreas, would you come immediately, please? The . . . the matter is urgent."

"Urgent?" Father Andreas said. Slowly and stiffly he got up. "Urgent?" he asked once more.

"Yes, it's the doctor. Doctor Cárdenas."

"Doctor Cárdenas," Father Andreas repeated. "Doctor Cárdenas? Oh, that one. Yes, of course. And what does Doctor Cárdenas want?"

"He is dead," the young priest said.

"What?" Father Andreas asked.

"This morning they found him. He . . . they say he was murdered."

"Murdered?"

"He was murdered," the young priest repeated. "The mayor and the judge have gone there already. And the police, of course. They asked if you would come immediately."

"Yes, yes, of course. Immediately," Father Andreas muttered, and shuffled out behind the young priest. In the street the heat assailed him. He could see that something extraordinary had happened. Everywhere in the village people stood in groups, talking excitedly.

"Look, there goes Father Andreas. Ave María Purísima," somebody said.

"I saw the mayor going there," added another.

"And the police."

"Yes, and the police!"

"How did it happen?"

"Shot," said a man. "Right through his head, so I heard."

"No, with a machete," someone else said.

"Of course, with a machete. A shot would have been heard!"

"True."

"The doctors' house is alone in that large garden with all those trees. . . ."

"And all the other doctors had gone home. Doctor Cárdenas was on duty. . . ."

"What a mess!"

"Who did it?"

"How should I know!"

"Maybe it was a woman."

"That could be! There were enough who. . . ."

"That's for sure. Aura, for instance!"

"Ah, Aura!"

"And Aura's father, Don Nepo, was not exactly fond of the doctor. . . ."

"Neither was Benita de Fátima. She would have liked Aura to. . . ."

"That's it. I can't blame her. Don Leonidas may be

old, but he has a lot of influence, and he's wealthy. What more can a girl wish for!"

"Yes, but that Aura was stuck on the doctor."

"And now she's saddled with his baby!"

"That's only too true."

"A few days ago someone saw Florinda with Doctor Cárdenas in his car."

"But I thought. . . ."

"It's true. He took her home!"

"Did he go in?"

"No, I don't think so. But he used to visit her quite often, as a doctor, I mean. Florinda is a nice girl and from a good family too. Nothing against her."

"No, no one talks against Florinda. That's true. But she must have been upset when . . . when the doctor and Aura. . . ."

"Yes, she took it badly, poor thing. It's not surprising that. . . ." The woman stopped abruptly and shook her head.

"That what?"

"I only have it from hearsay," the woman said hesitantly, "but she's been drinking of late!"

"Really! Drinking!"

"Yes. She never goes to the same shop twice, so no one will notice."

"Really, to hear that about Florinda! She must have been upset, poor thing, about the doctor and Aura!"

"But I thought that Lucindo went to Florinda's occasionally."

"To Florinda's? Come on! Lucindo is pining for Aura."

"He didn't have the slightest chance, at least as long as the doctor was alive, and he knew it."

"Yes, but now the doctor is dead!"

"Bless his soul!"

"I went to Lucindo the other day to ask when he would come and mend our leaking pipe. My husband can't do it. If a person doesn't have hands, what . . . . That day he was busy making a copper lizard, with a tail as straight and as sharp as a knife. . . ."

In front of the doctors' house many people were gathered. Claudio and Alirio were there too. They had seen old Father Andreas going in and a doctor from a nearby village.

The mayor and the judge walked back and forth along the tiled path that led to Doctor Cárdenas's quarters. The mayor was gesticulating wildly; Don Fabio had his hands behind his back and his chin on his chest. The mayor talked without pause.

Alirio nudged Claudio, nodding his head in their direction. "Let's see if we can hear what they're talking about," he whispered.

"How? That policeman in front of the gate won't let anyone through, I bet," Claudio answered.

"Ah, but I know a hole in the fence," Alirio said with a grin. "Coming?" Once inside, they sneaked back through the overgrown garden till they were near the house. There they could hear the words of the mayor and the judge clearly.

". . . with all the problems we have, we certainly need this one!" the mayor said with disgust.

Don Fabio sucked the air in between his teeth. "That's right," he agreed. "There's no lack of problems. Ave María!"

But the mayor, not even listening, followed his own train of thought. ". . . a stab through the heart. That's what the doctor said, a stab with a pointed object. He must have died immediately."

"Not a machete?"

"No, a thin, pointed object, I believe, and not a trace of a struggle. Stabbed in cold blood!"

"In his sleep."

"Yes, in his sleep."

"You don't need much strength for that," Don Fabio remarked.

"No, you have a point there. It could have been done by a woman quite as easily as by a man!"

"That doesn't make things easier," Don Fabio said dryly. "He knew quite a few women!"

The mayor sighed. "I'm thirsty," he said. "Let's go in." They went inside and helped themselves to the store of whiskey that Doctor Cárdenas no longer needed.

"A pity," Alirio whispered. "Now we can't hear them anymore." He hesitated a moment, then crawled carefully between the shrubs to the windows at the back of the house. The shutters of the living room were closed, but the bedroom shutters were tilted to let in some air.

Alirio peered inside. There was not much to see. On the bed was a still form covered with a sheet. The doctor from the other village was there, talking softly with Father Andreas. There were some people standing around. That was all!

"Can you see anything?" Claudio whispered.

Alirio shrugged. "Almost nothing. There's a sheet over it."

"Let me see!" Claudio peered inside this time. But as Alirio had said, he could hardly see anything.

Impatiently Alirio pulled his sleeve, and together they sneaked back the way they had come and joined the people on the road in front of the gate. As they were standing there the thought occurred to Alirio that his parents would not grieve for what had happened, at any rate his mother would not.

Now that Doctor Cárdenas was out of the way, maybe she could persuade Aura to work for Don Leonidas again. Don Leonidas was wealthy, and he was a widower. . . . One never could tell! If he married Aura, they might be better off at home. Now if Aura just had some sense. . . .

The boys lingered on. Toward noon a funeral car came to take the body away. Claudio and Alirio watched until it disappeared around a corner of the road.

16

They were heading for the plain where the cattle grazed. It lay below them, a long, narrow valley dotted with palms and bamboo trees, flanked by mountain ranges. Flowering shrubs and trees covered the slopes, and the streams carving their way down rocky beds were white with foam. The cattle seen from afar looked like white specks against the green.

They rode slowly through the cane fields, down narrow paths. They did not say much. Pilar looked happy. Her father had given in to her. Claudio, somewhat perplexed at the sudden order to accompany Pilar, had managed to tear off his red shirt before they left and wash himself under the splashing water at the *trapiche*. Then he put on his shirt again and combed his wet hair. Now they rode close together on the narrow path; sometimes the sweating horses touched.

Without getting off his horse, Claudio opened and closed the gates between the fields. The trip was long, but at last they were riding among the cattle in the valley.

"Have you been to the *vaquería* before?" Pilar asked.

"No, never." Claudio looked around. He did not know this part of the hacienda at all. "The cattle look healthy," he remarked.

"Yes, they're Father's hobby. He had bulls sent from France and crossed them with zebus. It's been difficult, but he gave me one of the calves a little while ago. I call her Pepita. She will have grown since I was here last. Do you think she'll recognize me?"

Claudio smiled. "No," he said. "I don't think so."

"I do," Pilar said, convinced. "When the calf was born, I came every day to look at her, and I'm going to start seeing her regularly again."

"Maybe she'll have changed so much that you won't recognize her either."

"Of course, I will," Pilar insisted. "She's my calf, isn't she? Anyway she's been branded and given the number 363." She looked around intently. "I don't see her with this herd. Maybe she'll be over on the other side of the *vaquería.*"

They rode through the tall grass and crossed a little river. "At least it's cooler here," Pilar said, as the horses waded through the water. "I'm thirsty. Let's go to the *vaquería* first and ask Daniel where Pepita is grazing. He's the head of the cowhands."

The stable was almost in the valley's center, in the curve of the river, where it was cool under the mango trees. In the fenced-off yard children played among the chickens, dogs, and pigs. When the dogs started to bark, a woman came out of a dark hut. Pilar and Claudio dismounted.

"Eh, Carmencita, how are you?" Pilar asked.

"What should I say, niña Pilar?" Carmencita said dully, pushing the dishevelled hair from her eyes with the back of her hand. "Fair as always. Just fair."

"And Daniel? Is he at home? And how are you?" Pilar said to one of the little boys, patting him on his head.

Frightened, he ran to his mother and hid behind her skirts. Carmencita pushed him forward again. "Say hello," she ordered her son. "Say hello nicely to niña Pilar, and to the gentleman too! Will you come in?" She preceded them into the hut, chasing a chicken off the wooden bench and another from the table.

"Bring some glasses. Hurry up!" she ordered her little daughters. On the rickety table was a large pitcher of *agua panela*. Carmencita chased the flies away from the rim and filled the glasses.

"Yes," she said, as she passed her work-soiled hand over the table, "I'm pleased to see you again. You haven't been here for a long time."

"No, not for some time," Pilar agreed.

"And the gentleman, is it his first time here?"

"We're going to look at the calf," Pilar said, not answering her.

"The calf?"

"Yes, Pepita, my calf."

"Ah, yes," Carmencita said vaguely.

They gulped down their drinks, and she refilled their glasses.

"It's hot," she said. "There's thunder almost every night, but the rain doesn't come. It's so hot and dry." She wiped the sweat from her forehead.

"And Daniel?" Pilar asked again. "Is Daniel around? I want him to go with us. He'll know exactly where Pepita is."

"Daniel?" repeated Carmencita. "No, he's not here."

"Is he with the cattle? Where can we find him?"

"Who knows?" Carmencita answered slowly. "He didn't feel well yesterday."

"What's the matter with him?"

Carmencita shrugged her shoulders. "Who knows?" she repeated again. "Last Saturday he felt so ill that he thought he was going to die."

"Maybe he was drunk," suggested Pilar.

"Drunk?" Carmencita echoed her. "How could he have been drunk? Seventeen beers was all he'd had."

Pilar and Claudio got up, and the children, who had crowded around them, moved back respectfully.

"The lemonade was good, Carmencita. We were thirsty. Thank you for everything."

"You're welcome. Sorry I have nothing better. Come again soon," said Carmencita.

"We'll go on and look for Daniel."

"I don't know if he's come back. If he has, he said he was going to look at the cattle."

"So he's *not* here?" Pilar said.

"He went to the village for medicine, as I said before," Carmencita answered. "He hasn't been well for some time, the poor man. And with all the work . . . ."

Pilar and Claudio rode away from the yard under the staring eyes of the children. Their mother leaned against the doorframe with her arms folded over her breasts.

"Mmm," Pilar said, when they were some distance away. "Daniel certainly takes a long time to get his medicine. It's noon already! If my father knew that he disappears like that and leaves everything untended, he'd be furious."

"Yes, I guess so," Claudio said noncommittally.

They roamed on through the valley among the cattle, searching for the calf. Pilar's forehead was beaded with sweat, and her blouse stuck to her body. She looked around. "It's strange that we haven't seen her yet," she said.

"What?" Claudio asked. He had forgotten about the calf and was looking at Pilar.

"It's strange, I said, that we haven't seen her."

"Maybe we'll find her farther on," Claudio said encouragingly.

"You think so?" She looked up at him. "She's very beautiful. Entirely white."

"In Boyacá we have black-and-white cattle called

Holstein. They're beautiful too," Claudio said to divert her thoughts.

"Yes," Pilar answered. They rode on in silence, but still did not find the calf with the brand number 363. Pilar's face was woebegone, and Claudio began to worry too.

"Pepita," Pilar said softly.

"Three-six-three," Claudio added.

They looked at each other, smiling, and the tension broke.

"You remembered the number! It must be an easy one."

"I would remember Pepita's number."

"But you don't even know her."

"But I know you, and Pepita belongs to you!"

"That sounds much too complicated to me!" Pilar said, as she spurred on her horse. She rode off at a gallop across the plain, her long hair streaming in the wind.

Claudio watched her go until she almost had disappeared in the hazy distance. Anxiously he began to search among the cattle again. He wanted to find the calf for her. They did not have much time, for soon it would be too dark to make out the numbers. His eyes swept over the heifers, the yearlings, the calves.

Then he heard her galloping back toward him. Pilar pulled up at his side. "Any luck?" she asked anxiously.

"No, not yet."

"You don't think, you don't think she's been stolen?" Her eyes looked frightened.

"Oh, no." Claudio looked around. "This valley is pretty well protected," he said, with as much confidence as he could muster.

"Yes, but still. . . ." She kept looking at him, her eyes round.

He couldn't think of anythng more to say, for of course the calf might have been stolen. "Let's make a circle again and have another look," he said at last.

They rode on. The shadows of the palm trees lengthened, and the valleys, between the spurs of the mountains, were blue with haze. In the silence only the irregular *clop, clop* of hooves was audible. Now and then their knees brushed. As they rode, Pilar peered down at the cattle, examining each calf that they passed. Claudio's eyes searched the mountain ridges. There probably were many paths along the rivers and among the trees. Suddenly he noticed the *chulus*, the vultures, circling over something.

"You stay here for moment," he said to Pilar. "It's getting late. I'm going to look a little further."

He spurred on his horse and rode away. Near a tree clump he checked his horse so sharply that it reared. Big black vultures slowly flew away. Some settled on the branches of a dead tree nearby, stretching their naked necks. Others moved into the tall grass, flapping their wings.

Claudio looked down. There. . . .

"Claudio!" Pilar's voice broke the silence. "Claudio!"

He didn't answer. He didn't dare to look around. Then he heard her horse galloping toward him. "I'm coming," he yelled, but he was too late. With a jerk she pulled up the bay beside him.

"Claudio, what. . . ?" Then, hardly breathing, she whispered, "Oh," slipped from her horse, and knelt on the ground next to the dead calf.

"Oh," she said again. "Pepita! It's not true." She bent over the calf. Her honey-colored hair fell like a waterfall onto the dull gleam of the white body. "Tell me it isn't true."

Claudio dismounted. He knelt beside her without a word and looked at the calf. He wished he could tell her that it wasn't true. He wanted to comfort her, but did not know how. His hand reached out and his fingers became entangled in her blond hair.

They sat there for a long time. Around them the dusk fell, and the stars began to glow in the smoldering green evening sky.

17

Florinda rocked gently in her chair on the terrace at the back of her house, staring with unseeing eyes over the balustrade and down into the flower-filled garden. She had opened the window on the street side of the house to let the breeze blow through. It was suffocatingly hot, even in the evening. Then she had installed herself in back, the bottle and the glass on the table before her. She might just as well stay there. Waiting at the window on the street was pointless. There was not much left to wait for.

". . . only death," Florinda said aloud.

A door creaked and Nubia appeared. "You want something, Doña Florinda?"

"What did you say?"

"I thought you called me. I heard you speak."

"No, my child, I didn't say anything," Florinda said impatiently. "Go to bed."

Nubia withdrew into her room, but left the door ajar to get some air. Tomorrow she would try to go back to her mother; she would ask her if she couldn't work somewhere else. Doña Florinda was acting very strangely lately. She talked to herself and she was drinking. Nubia had noticed the bottle. Yes, she wanted to leave. Tomorrow she would make an excuse and get away.

Outside there sounded the raucous blare of a car horn. Florinda gave a start, stiffened, and then leaned back again. "It's nothing, only a taxi probably," she muttered, smiling to herself. Was she crazy? Alvaro was dead, wasn't he? And she was better off, yes, much better! How many evenings had she waited like a fool? Now she was at peace, and Aura had not won him either! Yes, things were better this way. She smiled, reaching for the bottle, then stopped with her hand in midair. The feeling came over her that someone outside was watching her. She didn't want to turn around, but at last she did. On the other side of the grilled window, she saw the dark outline of a man. Someone in the street was looking in. She got up and went slowly through the room.

"Oh, it's you, she said, relieved.

"Yes," answered Lucindo. "It's me. I, I happened to be passing by, and I noticed you sitting there."

Of course, that was not true. Florinda knew he could not have seen her, if he had not stopped and looked inside. Well, someone had come at least.

"Wait," she said. "Wait, I'll open the door!" Quickly she went to the door, and Lucindo entered in his usual hesitating way.

"I'm sitting outside," Florinda said. "On the terrace. It's cooler there."

"It is hot," Lucindo acknowledged. "Very hot and oppressive. It's time for the rains to come." There was a blue flicker of lightning, and for a moment the garden was illuminated.

Florinda pulled over a chair. "I have cold beer," she said. "Would you like beer or . . . or maybe some whiskey? This bottle was a present from Doctor Cárdenas."

"Ah yes, Doctor Cárdenas," Lucindo said. "That was really something!"

"Yes, yes," Florinda said hurriedly. She did not want to think of him.

"The entire village is talking about nothing else."

"I don't mingle much with people here, but I can imagine. Do they know who did it?"

"There are rumors," Lucindo answered softly. "One never can tell." He hesitated, and then added, "This afternoon there was quite a fight, on the corner by the drugstore, where Don Nepo sells his lottery tickets."

"Really?"

"The man who works for the druggist, the one with the bad hands who still plays the best billiards in the village, dropped a remark about Benita de Fátima. 'Now your wife will get her way,' he said. That's all. But Don Nepo didn't like it, and they went for each other. Half the village got mixed up in it. After all, everybody knows that Benita de Fátima wanted Aura to. . . ." Lucindo fell silent, shaking his head a little sadly.

"Aura!" Florinda repeated, and she sniffed in contempt.

Lucindo thought of the beetle that he had turned into a brooch for Aura. It had been hard work, and for what? Even though the doctor was out of the way, Aura still ignored him. Making the gift had been in vain. He put his hand in his pocket.

"There are cigarettes here," Florinda said, pushing a pack toward him.

But Lucindo pulled out an oblong parcel, wrapped in newspaper. "Here, this is for you," he said.

"For me?" She unwrapped the parcel slowly. "But," she said, "but. . . ." She was obviously astonished. "Did your really make that?" she asked with awe.

Lucindo nodded.

"Beautiful," she said. "Beautiful!" She turned the exquisitely worked copper lizard with its long, pointed tail slowly in her hands. "Those eyes are like emeralds."

"You may have it," Lucindo said. "I brought it for you, if you like it."

"Oh, it's really beautiful. But, but it must have taken such a long time."

Lucindo shrugged his shoulders. "I'll be making something else soon," he said carelessly.

Florinda got up. She fetched water and ice from the

refrigerator and poured whiskey for Lucindo. Then she lighted the table lamp.

Through a slit in the door Nubia watched the scene with curiosity. She had never seen Lucindo here before. The doctor, yes, but Lucindo? And what were the two of them looking at? It was a pointed object. The doctor had been stabbed. He hadn't been killed with a machete, they had said. Tomorrow she would leave for certain. The whole village knew that her *patrona* had eyes for the doctor, and Lucindo had been after Aura. That everybody also knew. And Aura and the doctor. . . . Now the doctor was dead, and Doña Florinda and Lucindo sat together on the terrace, that sharp, shiny thing between them. . . . She would have liked to leave right away, but she did not dare. Softly she closed the door. Shuddering with fright, she crawled into bed and pulled the sheet over her head.

Florinda and Lucindo sat silently side by side, in the rocking chairs, drinking their whiskey. Florinda gulped hers down greedily. Lucindo drank slowly. He was not accustomed to it; in fact, he did not like it. He would have preferred beer.

"Would you like another one?"

"No, thank you. I must go."

"Already? But you've just come."

Florinda suddenly realized that she liked Lucindo's presence, even though he didn't say as much as Alvaro. But that was all finished. Lucindo was the one who sat here now beside her. Maybe he was lonely, too, as she was. My God, so lonely. And Lucindo was alone, with only a sick old mother, who was not much company.

Lucindo rose to his feet. "Well, I'll be going," he said in his soft, gentle voice.

Florinda remained seated, hoping to delay his departure. "You'll come again soon?" she asked.

"Yes," Lucindo answered. "I'll do that."

"It's a pity you have to go. How is your mother? You didn't tell me about her."

"Ah, my mother," Lucindo answered softly. "She sent her greetings. She died last week."

18

"Do they know who did it yet?" Don Leonidas asked, looking at the judge.

Don Fabio shook his head. "Don't talk about it!" he answered irritably. "We're making no headway at all. Of course, there are plenty of rumors. But proof, no. Everything has been handled in the stupidest way possible right from the beginning. The servant girl who found him brought half the village to the scene with her screams, before anyone even thought of informing the authorities. By the time we arrived, the entire place was filled with people who had no business there. The fellow who did it could have been there among them! Everybody has a different story. "

"Yes, that's true," Don Leonidas agreed. "I hear the strangest things. Someone even mentioned that Don Nepo, Aura's father. . . ."

"Oh, that's the only thing that we're sure of," Don Fabio interrupted him.

"What do you mean?" Don Leonidas asked sharply.

"That he was not killed for money. So far nothing

of value seems to be missing. So the motive must be revenge."

"Well, there were plenty of people who didn't like him," Don Leonidas said contemptuously. "That's for sure!"

"Yes, yes!" Don Fabio answered impatiently. "But everyone here knows everything about everybody! Anyone could have done it. Everyone knew that the other doctors weren't there, everyone knew that Cárdenas was on duty, and everyone seems to have known that he didn't take the trouble to lock his door." Don Fabio began to get excited. "Imagine, going to bed without locking the door. Anyone could get in. It's up to us to find out who did!" Don Fabio sighed heavily.

"Yes, an official has to earn his living once in a while," Don Leonidas remarked, looking mockingly at Don Fabio's angry face. "Claudio, go and get the whiskey."

"By the way I did find out one thing," Don Fabio said.

"What's that?"

"I know who that property belongs to."

"That property?"

"The property at the river, between those two lots of yours."

"Ah, yes," Don Leonidas said with interest. He leaned forward in his chair, one sinewy hand patting the trousers pinned together where the feet should have been. He looked at the judge. "Who?" he asked.

"You won't be happy about it, I'm afraid," Don Fabio said with exasperating slowness.

"Who?" Don Leonidas repeated frigidly. He didn't like being kept waiting for information.

"To Doña Ana Eugenia."

There was a silence.

"To Doña Ana Eugenia. Well, well," Don Leonidas finally repeated slowly. He frowned.

"I said you wouldn't be happy with the news," Don Fabio repeated, signaling Claudio to fill his glass.

Don Leonidas stared for a moment into space. "Of course, we could try to buy it," he said. "What use is that piece of land to that woman?"

"Yes, of course, you could try." Don Fabio's voice did not sound very optimistic. "But I doubt whether she'll be interested."

"Maybe she's forgotten that she owns the property," Don Leonidas said thoughtfully. "From what I hear, she's not in her right mind."

"You might be wrong there. Doctor Cárdenas always said. . . ." Don Fabio stopped short. He had not meant to start talking again about the doctor. He'd been occupied all day long with nothing else, and the sarcastic remark that Don Leonidas had made a while ago upset him. "After all, how would that help you," he added.

"Well, everything can be settled somehow, one way or another," Don Leonidas said confidently. "The druggist at the corner fired his man who insulted Don Nepo. Did you know that?"

"No, I didn't know that the druggist and Don Nepo were such good friends."

"Ah, but the druggist is well aware that he rents the premises from me! That is to say, when I reminded him of it, he immediately understood."

"Ah," said Don Fabio. "I see."

"So I send Alirio to take the job. He's been fed up with working at Puerta Grande for some time, and he was glad to make a change. I believe he's started already. At least, that's what Aura said." Don Leonidas tapped his cane softly on the tiles. He looked pleased.

"That's all well and good, but what has it got to do with Doña Ana Eugenia? She doesn't live in a house of yours, does she?"

"No," Don Leonidas answered. "She doesn't live in a house of mine. . . ."

"And I don't think that she'll be coming to you to borrow money, will she? She has plenty, I believe."

"No, she doesn't live in a house of mine. . . ." Don Leonidas repeated thoughtfully. "I wouldn't permit her to smear green paint on the walls of a house of mine. Such a person belongs in an asylum, don't you agree?"

Don Fabio shrugged. "Even then. . . ." he said. "What would you gain? No, the best you can do is put this boy here—what's his name, Claudio?—and his father—Don Pacho, eh?—in Marta Mesa's little house."

"Mmmmm." Don Leonidas thought over the plan. Don Fabio had suggested it before, and maybe it was not such a bad idea at that. Claudio could work for him instead of going to Puerta Grande. He could live over there by the river and cultivate the land. Don Pacho could go with him. Now that Aura was coming regularly to do the housekeeping, he could do without the company of Don Pacho, who seemed to be getting a lot worse lately.

"Mmmm," he murmured again. "Maybe you're right. At any rate, Claudio could start working on those two lots for me. And that property, that property of Doña Ana Eugenia's—we must think of something!"

His cane tapped the tiles again, and he did not look so pleased anymore. "Think about it," he said to Don Fabio. "Claudio, more whiskey!"

Don Fabio didn't answer. He had something else to think about right now. The doctor's murder.

Claudio brought the whiskey, and then went slowly to the room where his father sat in the dark on the edge of his bed. He burned with rage. Those two were deciding his future without even asking him. He didn't want to work for Don Leonidas at all. He wanted to stay at Puerta Grande.

"Did you hear?" he asked his father softly.

Don Pacho nodded. "Yes," he said listlessly.

"I don't want to work for Don Leonidas," Claudio said flatly.

"We must leave here," Don Pacho answered. "We are in the way."

"I'm not going to get stuck in Marta Mesa's house, tilling that plot by the river. I'm not going to work for nothing, and he won't pay us."

"No," Don Pacho said. In a low voice he continued, "It would be best if you returned to Boyacá. To the *finca*. . . ."

Claudio didn't answer. He didn't want to return to Boyacá either.

"I should never have brought you here," Don Pacho said. He shook his head sadly. "No, I shouldn't have done that. This is no environment for a young healthy boy like you! You must go back to Boyacá!"

"And you?" Claudio asked.

"I'm old and sick. Maybe they'll take me into the hospital." He nodded hopefully and tried to believe what he was suggesting. They had become superfluous in this house when Aura began to come regularly. She didn't do much, but when she was there Don Leonidas followed her with his eyes. When she disappeared from his view, he started tapping his cane on the tiles angrily. As long as Aura was around, Don Leonidas didn't listen to his stories.

"We must leave here. It's better if we go," the old man repeated.

"But I don't want to leave," Claudio said stubbornly. "I want to stay here."

He thought of Pilar, whom he saw regularly. Now that Alirio didn't work at Puerta Grande anymore, he could meet her in the evening after work more easily. No, he didn't want to leave. He wanted to stay at Puerta Grande near Pilar. But he clearly understood that standing up to Don Leonidas would be difficult. His father was right. It was better to go.

19

The water ran gurgling over the rocks, the bright night shimmered through the fern fronds. Darkness gathered in the tall grass around them so that they hardly could make out the far edge of the stream. But the flat rock on which they sat was still warm from the sun. Then the green light, sifting through the fanlike leaves, changed to luminous blue as lightning flashed across the sky. Fireflies floated in the air, and cicadas chorused their shrill song.

"Why don't you want me to go there on my own?" Pilar asked. Her nose wrinkled as she frowned.

"Because. . . ." Claudio answered. "Oh, I can't explain it very well."

"I like to go to the lake. It's quiet there and beautiful."

"There are plenty of other beautiful spots."

"Not where I can swim."

"You can swim in the pool."

"That's what my grandmother says, and Albertina," Pilar said, pouting.

"Of course, they love you too."

"Too?" Pilar looked at him.

Claudio gazed silently at the swiftly running stream, a silvery ribbon between the dark banks. "Promise me that you won't go there alone."

"Why should I promise that?"

"The lake is deep. Some parts are very deep, and then there are all those weeds!"

"It's because of those stories that Miguel Angel, el Indio, always tells," Pilar said. "I know. But you said yourself that they were nonsense."

Claudio kept silent. He couldn't possibly tell her that now he thought maybe they were true. He had seen the woman with his own eyes, there, near the lake, that night when he went to Puerta Grande. He didn't know what to think yet. If he told her about his experience, she would ask him why he had come to their house in the middle of the night. For that, too, he had no explanation.

"And if we go together?" Pilar asked.

"That would be all right, but I don't know how long I'll ... I. ..." Claudio hastily swallowed his last words.

Pilar sat up straight, turning her narrow face toward him. She looked frightened as she had that day at the lake and the time when they had looked for the calf in the valley.

"You're not going away, are you?" she asked him, her voice low.

"Yes, maybe, I don't know. Maybe I'm going back to Boyacá."

"Why?"

"Because I have to," Claudio said shortly.

Pilar gazed into the darkness. Her hands, clasped about her knees, tightened. "So you're leaving here," she said, trying hard to be matter-of-fact.

Claudio leaned toward her, and his shoulder touched hers. "I'll come back," he said seriously. "I promise you that I will. Do you believe me?"

"Yes," Pilar said.

"Don't say anything to anyone, though, not just yet."

"To whom? Who do you mean?" She looked at him.

"To your father. Or to Nestor. I . . . I'm not leaving right away. It will be some time yet."

"When then?" Pilar persisted, her words barely audible. She just had found someone, she thought, someone she could talk to, and who would listen to her. She could tell him everything, almost everything, and now. . . .

Pilar stared at the white, foaming water. It ran swiftly between the banks, and she could not stop it. "When are you going?" she repeated, looking at him again.

"I don't know," Claudio said hesitantly. He wished fervently he could tell her everything, even about the village. But he knew he could not. Even though he was healthy, he could not tell her anything about where he came from. As long as he lived in the village, he was marked like the rest of them, like all those people with their frightful illness, their disfigured faces, their stumps of arms, and their misshapen feet. I'll stay until my father is in the hospital, he thought. And then I'll tell Don Leonidas that I won't be working his land by the river, because I'm leaving! His father had been right. He should not stay in the village when he was young and vigorous and healthy. He could work anywhere, and he could earn money. Then, when he was settled, he would return to Puerta Grande.

"Is it true, what you said a while ago?" Pilar asked in a tiny voice.

"What's that?"

"About that 'too.' "

He looked down at her and smiled. "Yes," he said.

"And you have a reason to warn me about the lake."

"Yes, I have."

"Then I won't go there again, not on my own at least. . . . But we can go together as long as you're here," she added quickly.

"Yes."

Lightning flashed. For a moment they sat silent. Their faces were illumined by the blue quivering glow, and they listened for the distant rolling thunder.

"I must go home," Pilar said at last, "or my grandmother will be angry again. And Albertina too." The frown was back on her face.

Claudio reached for the overhanging ferns and gently touched her face with a green lacy leaf, erasing the unhappy expression. They laughed. The leaf slipped from his hand and swept upward toward the sky, scattering the stars. Once again the night flashed electric blue, and over the cane fields came the dark rumble of thunder.

2O

Don Pacho was sitting on his bed. The yellow shoes in which he had been married three times were under it, and the chicken he had trained perched beside him. Through the open door he could see the wide, tiled back porch where Aura was at work. She was sweeping carelessly, not watching what she was doing. As Claudio crossed the patio Aura stopped her work and looked at him. He had just bathed and was bare from the waist up, a ragged towel draped across his shoulders. Leaning on her broom, she smiled at him.

"How are you?" she asked. "How's everything?"

"Fine," Claudio answered. "How's Alirio? I haven't seen him for a while."

"Alirio is all right." Aura smiled again. "He's making more money than at Puerta Grande, he says. He likes the work better, he has a bicycle, and he has more time off."

"I returned the machete," Claudio said.

"Don't you need it anymore? I heard that you're

162

going to work for Don Leonidas on his land down by the river."

"I bought one myself," Claudio said evasively.

From the dark interior of the house, Don Leonidas appeared, wheeling his chair. "Aura," he called. "Aura. . . ."

"Yes," Aura answered. "Yes, I'm here." She winked at Claudio and started sweeping again slowly, a smile curving on her wide mouth. She did not look up when Don Leonidas drew near, but continued to sweep.

Claudio slipped into the room where his father sat. "How are you?" he asked.

"Fair," Don Pacho answered. He looked old and worn. "Today I went to the head of the health service in the village. It wasn't easy for me. His office is far, and the roads are bad. I can't walk well anymore, not as before. . . ."

"What did he say?" Claudio interrupted.

"He'll try. Perhaps they'll take me, he says." Don Pacho nodded. "That will be better," he added. "We must leave here."

"Yes," Claudio agreed, taking the new machete that he had bought with his own money from under his bed. He passed his thumb along the razor-sharp blade. "Did you notice Aura just now?" he asked.

"You'd better not talk much with Aura," the old man answered. "Don Leonidas doesn't like it. Don't have much to do with her, my son."

Claudio shrugged. "What can I do?" he said. "She starts the conversation, and she is Alirio's sister after all."

"You'd better not," his father said again. Claudio was silent and started to dress. He knew that his father was right.

The atmosphere was tense in the house of late. Almost anything threw Don Leonidas into a temper. He worried about his property by the river and brooded about the land that was not his, puzzling how to get his hands on it. He wanted that land. The idea was constantly on his mind. Sometimes he didn't even notice when Aura said good-night and disappeared among the shadowy trees, sleek and supple as a lynx. Lost in thought, he sat in the yellow light of the naked bulb that dangled on a cord from the ceiling.

"That land," Don Leonidas said between his teeth. His hands whitened on his cane, and his muscles tensed. What use was that land to Doña Ana Eugenia? She would never do anything with it. But Don Fabio said that she didn't want to sell it either. If he only could acquire that land, his river property would be much more valuable and easier to cultivate. Claudio could work the whole piece. He and his father could live over there, and he would be rid of them in the house. Don Leonidas grinned. He was fed up with them. The old man was no longer useful. And Claudio? He must keep an eye on him. He had seen Aura smile at him. Aura! He looked around with suspicion.

Aura had gone and left her broom leaning against the wall.

"Claudio!" Don Leonidas called, tapping his cane angrily. "Claudio!"

There was the sound of steps on the path beside the house, and Don Fabio appeared in the circle of light on the porch.

"Ah," Don Leonidas said. "It's you. What is the news? Did you hear from Doña Ana Eugenia? Did you go there yourself as I told you to do?"

"Yes," Don Fabio said, sucking in air between his teeth.

"And?"

"Just as I thought," Don Fabio answered. "She wouldn't receive me. She doesn't receive anyone."

"Mmmm," Don Leonidas muttered. He looked annoyed.

"I expected that, of course," Don Fabio continued slowly. "She only received that Doctor Cárdenas. He went there occasionally."

"But Doctor Cárdenas is dead," Don Leonidas said. "That's no good."

"Yes, Doctor Cárdenas is dead," Don Fabio repeated. "Murdered," he added with a significant glance.

"What's that got to do with it?" Don Leonidas said. "Claudio, where are you?" He rapped angrily on the floor. "Bring the whiskey."

Claudio was sitting in the dark with his father. Because Don Fabio had come, Claudio hadn't answered Don Leonidas's first call, but now he went to the sitting room to serve the whiskey.

Again Don Fabio sucked in air between his teeth. "Doctor Cárdenas is murdered, and I'm in charge of the investigation, as you know," he said caustically.

"Yes, yes. What's that to do with Doña Ana Eugenia?" Don Leonidas asked.

"I don't know yet exactly," Don Fabio answered, with a slight smile. "But I did find something very interesting in the doctor's house. Look at this." He pulled something from his pocket and handed it to Don Leonidas. It was a finger-smeared photograph.

Claudio stood inside the open door, beside the crate of whiskey, and he could see the picture plainly. It was a photograph of Pilar with Dagmé.

Don Leonidas held the picture in his sinewy hands for a long time and looked at it carefully. Then he said with contempt, "A most remarkable discovery! Our dear doctor seems to have had quite a collection. But so what?"

Don Fabio was not put off. "Ah," he said, amused. "But I don't think that this one belongs to the doctor's collection. She's not a girl from the village, as you can see."

"No," Don Leonidas agreed. "No, she isn't. In fact, I don't know who she is."

"But I do," Don Fabio said, taking the glass of whiskey from Claudio. He looked as pleased with himself as a cat with a mouse, and he didn't notice Claudio's trembling hand.

"Well, congratulations," Don Leonidas said without interest. He dropped the picture on his knee and tapped his cane on the tiles.

"Perhaps you should look at what is written on the back," Don Fabio recommended.

Don Leonidas turned the picture over and started to read. His lips moved as he spelled out the words. Slowly he said out loud, "Pilar, my daughter."

Don Fabio nodded with approval. "Exactly," he said. "That's what it says. 'Pilar, my daughter.' And the photograph is smeared with green paint. His voice was loaded with implication. "As green as the rooms at Doña Ana Eugenia's."

"But," Don Leonidas started.

"I should be able to prove that the fingerprints are those of Doña Ana Eugenia quite easily," Don Fabio continued. "And the handwriting too, no doubt, since it isn't the doctor's. Yes, I should be able to prove that this picture belongs to her quite easily."

"But," Don Leonidas started again. "I never knew she had a daughter."

"Neither did I," Don Fabio agreed. "But Doctor Cárdenas evidently knew. He went there on sick calls, remember. He must have seen the picture there and taken it."

"Taken it?" Don Leonidas repeated. "Taken it."

He dwelled on the words, his brain working feverishly. "Why would he have taken the picture?" he asked.

"It seems pretty clear to me," Don Fabio answered. "The doctors here don't earn much. Doctor Cárdenas discovered Doña Ana Eugenia's secret, and Doña Ana Eugenia has money. A little gold mine!"

"A little gold mine is right," Don Leonidas said. "Well, he didn't enjoy it for long."

"That's true."

Don Leonidas didn't move, but stared intently at Don Fabio's face. Finally he said, "Are you claiming that. . . ?"

"I'm not claiming anything," Don Fabio interrupted.

"Poor thing," Don Leonidas said with compassion. Don Fabio pretended that he had not heard that last remark, and Don Leonidas, suddenly vehement, continued, "Her child was at stake, you realize. That wretched doctor would have sucked up her last penny, with the picture of her daughter in his possession. She wanted it back. Doctor Cárdenas never knew what happened to him. He sat there, fast asleep. The knife went into him like jelly. She must have been at her wit's end. He would have squeezed her to her last penny, even to the piece of land . . . the land. . . ." Don Leonidas stopped short. He slid the photograph into his pocket. He shook his head again. "The poor creature," he repeated.

Don Fabio wiped his yellow face with his hand. "At any rate, it introduces a new angle into the case," he said evenly. "Though"—he hesitated—"I wonder where she got the strength."

"You must take into account that she was not in her right mind," Don Leonidas said. "Those people are sometimes stronger than they know themselves." He gazed into his glass of whiskey. "Well, well, who would have thought it?" he muttered.

Claudio sneaked away. In his room he lay down on his bed, his machete beside him. His thumb passed over the sharp blade again and again. He was burning with an almost uncontrollable rage. Those two hyenas, sitting there drinking on the back porch, talking about Pilar. Pilar and Doña Ana Eugenia. Pilar and her mother! It couldn't be true. . . .

But why didn't Don Manuel want to employ anyone from the village? Why didn't Doña Ana Eugenia ever receive anyone? Why was Pilar frightened sometimes by the feeling that someone was near her at night? What about the woman he had seen at the lake? Everything fell into place.

But if it was true, then he must warn Pilar. He must protect her against the terrible things that she would have to go through. The secret would come out, and everybody would be talking about it!

He was the only one who could help her. Tonight? No, it was too late now. He would wait until he could talk to her calmly, to prepare her. But he must not wait too long. Time was precious. Tomorrow afternoon maybe? After work they could go to the lake, and there in the green dusk of the trees he would tell her. He would urge her to come with him, away from here, away from this stinking village, away from Puerta Grande with its horrible secret, away from the terrible things that were about to happen. There would be a trial to establish who had murdered Doctor Cárdenas, that much was certain.

He was young and strong, though. He would work for her. Claudio's face lighted up. Tomorrow. . . .

On the back porch Don Leonidas said thoughtfully, "It's about time that I put Claudio to work on my land. And when I have that other plot as well. . . ."

"Does he still work at Puerta Grande?" Don Fabio asked.

"Yes, but that can be handled," Don Leonidas answered confidently. "I didn't get Alirio that job at the druggist's for nothing. Alirio is a good boy, who owes much to me. Alirio will be quite willing to go on an errand for an old man like me."

21

Nestor had left after telling him to supervise the work-
men. Slowly Claudio rode through the cane fields. But
he did not see the working hands or the cane that fell
under the machetes. The only thing he saw was Pilar's
face.

How can I tell her? he thought. How can I tell her
about Doña Ana Eugenia, who lives in the village and
is ill? Her own mother, her own mother, who has
. . . . Worst of all, how can I tell her about the murder
of Doctor Cárdenas?

Doña Ana Eugenia? She must have been out of her
mind as Don Leonidas had said. Doctor Cárdenas had
been full of wicked tricks with his girls, like Florinda,
for example. But Florinda had not been his girl really,
not the way Aura was. Aura, that little serpent. . . . If
only his father could be admitted to the hospital soon.
He must talk to Pilar. Today, tonight. He had not
caught sight of her yet today and realized that he was
avoiding her purposely.

Claudio dreaded the encounter, for he did not know

what to say or how to begin. First he would tell her that she must not be upset. Perhaps if he began with his father? Yes, he would say that his father was also ill. Maybe that would comfort her, and then she would not feel ashamed. But that other matter. . . . Maybe he didn't have to tell her. The two of them could be far away before the scandal broke. Later, if she did find out, he always could say that Don Fabio and Don Leonidas were lying to cover up something, because Don Leonidas wanted that plot of land. Just as he wanted Aura too! Don Leonidas was a man of influence, used to getting his way. Usually he did get his way as Aura was proving. Who would have thought that Aura. . . ? Aura was beautiful and young and irresistible. If Doctor Cárdenas were still alive, perhaps Aura would have caught him in the end, and Don Leonidas would have been left out of the picture.

But Doctor Cárdenas was dead, murdered in his sleep. What was it again that Don Leonidas had said?

"The knife went into him like jelly." He had not known what was happening to him, sitting there, fast asleep! But Doctor Cárdenas had been found on his bed, as far as everybody knew! And how did Don Leonidas know the way the knife went in? The knife? What knife? They were still looking for the weapon. Already they had gone to Lucindo in his workshop and asked for the lizard he had made. Then they had gone to Florinda's and taken the lizard away! Everybody knew that. But a lizard was not a knife.

"What knife was he talking about?" Claudio said out loud. Images moved in front of his eyes, images merging one into another. Doctor Cárdenas, young, vigorous, and healthy. Aura, the beautiful Aura. Don Leonidas never would have got her if. . . .

Claudio turned his horse abruptly. He had to be sure. He galloped through the hills and back to the yard. Dismounting, he looked around. Nestor would be furious if he found out that he had left his work. No matter, they would be leaving. . . .

He caught sight of Pilar on the veranda of the house. She saw him too. Turning away, she called, "Albertina, I'm going for a swim soon. Where is my bathing suit?" Then she looked back at Claudio, and he made a small answering gesture with his hand. They understood each other.

Claudio ran downhill as fast as he could. He forgot to take the roundabout way through Palo Quemado, as he always did, but ran straight for the village. He had to be sure as quickly as possible. Then he would go to the lake, where Pilar would be waiting for him!

Claudio was so intent on the problem he was working out in his mind that he saw little on either side of him. He certainly did not notice Alirio on his bicycle, bent low over the handlebars, leaving the village by the road that led to Puerta Grande by way of Palo Quemado.

Out of breath, trembling all over, Claudio came to a stop in front of Don Leonidas's house. All of a sudden he felt less sure. He didn't know how to handle the situation. He hesitated for a moment, then softly sneaked around the house. At this time of day the heat was at its worst, and everything was heavy and still. Everyone retired into the comparative coolness of his heavy-walled house.

The door of the room where he slept with his father was ajar. He could hear the heavy, irregular breathing of the old man. The door to the large, cheerless sitting room, where the beer cartons and the crate of whiskey stood against the wall, was also open. But the door to Don Leonidas's room was closed. Don Leonidas was not around and neither was Aura. The wheelchair was in front of the door to the bedroom, and Don Leonidas's cane lay across it.

Claudio crept toward it. Without a sound he took the cane, and with all his force he swung it through the air. It opened and the little razor-sharp knife flicked out. It was a horrible weapon.

Quickly Claudio slid the cane through his hands and stared at the pointed knife. Then he scraped it with his nail. There was dried blood on the tip.

Claudio closed his eyes for a moment. It was true then! In his mind's eye he could see Don Leonidas, with the dexterity of a cat, maneuvering his wheelchair through the house and down the dark road to the doctor's home. Doctor Cárdenas had fallen asleep in his chair. One thrust with his cane, and it was over. Maybe Doctor Cárdenas had not even awakened. Don

Leonidas could have lifted him without much effort in those strong arms of his and trundled him, across the arms of his wheelchair, into the bedroom. The murder could have happened that way. He was almost sure it had.

Claudio heard a slight noise in the other room. He had just enough time to hide the cane behind the crates of beer, when the bedroom door opened. Aura came out, her feet bare. She was wearing a pink wrapper, which she held with one hand. She half shut the door behind her.

"Oh, it's you," she said.

"Yes."

"Where did you come from all of a sudden?"

"I . . . from nowhere . . . from Puerta Grande." Claudio was stuttering.

"Ah," Aura said. She laughed mockingly. "So early?" she asked.

"Yes, but I must go back," Claudio said hurriedly.

Aura raised her eyebrows. "Ah," she said again. Then in a softer voice she added, "Shall I see you tonight?" She looked at him through half-closed eyelids, her lips slightly parted.

Claudio didn't answer. From the bedroom came the sound of Don Leonidas's voice, short and impatient. "Aura!"

"Ah," Aura said again. Her eyes were slits. She turned back toward the room in her pink wrapper and on naked feet. "I'm coming," she called. "I'm bringing you your chair!" She wheeled it through the door into the bedroom.

"Who's there? Who were you talking to?" asked Don Leonidas sharply.

"Me? With Don Pacho," Aura said, closing the door with her foot.

Claudio grabbed the cane and disappeared in a flash. Fortunately, Aura, the little bitch, had not noticed anything. But Don Leonidas certainly would miss it right away. There was not much time. He must hurry.

Again he went through the quiet village. People were inside, in the somewhat cooler shadows of the dark houses. Nevertheless, anyone might be watching him. Claudio tried to carry the cane as inconspicuously as possible. He didn't know what he should do with it or to whom he should take it. Don Fabio? Certainly not. He did not trust Don Fabio one inch. The mayor? But the mayor was a friend of Don Fabio's. At any rate, they knew each other. Father Andreas? Yes, Father Andreas. That was an idea. But, no, Father Andreas was old. Old and absentminded. Father Andreas might not understand and send him on to Don Fabio with his story. So he would not go to him. But then to whom?

Claudio shrugged off the difficult question. He could not bother about that now. He had to go to the lake, to Pilar, who was waiting for him.

Claudio began to run. Far in the distance he could see the bluish outline of the trees around the lake.

Pilar would be sitting there on the tree stump at the water's edge, the way she always sat, with her arms around her legs.

Suddenly he narrowed his eyes, protecting them with his free hand to keep out the glare. On the narrow, well-trodden path Pilar came riding. She rode very slowly, and her eyes were fixed on Claudio. When they were quite near, Pilar checked her horse and Claudio stopped too.

"So it's true," Pilar said. Her eyes flashed icily at him.

"Is what true?" Claudio asked. He never had seen her eyes that blue before.

"It's true . . . what Alirio told us. That you live in that stinking village, with all those people who are rotting away. And you always told me that you came from Boyacá, that you have a *finca* there . . . that . . . and that. . . ."

"But we do," said Claudio. "It's true. We do have a *finca* in Boyacá."

Pilar's lips curled in contempt. "Your father is ill," she said, her voice hoarse with anger. "Your father is ill, and the man you live with is ill as well! You have lived there all the time, with those sick men, and you have touched me. . . . You. . . ."

She raised her hand, and her whip whistled through the air, striking Claudio on the side of his face. Dazed, he raised his hand, the hand with the cane. It dropped to the ground, and he wiped his cheek.

"You liar," Pilar said softly with a trembling voice.
"Just so you know that you cannot fool me, with your
finca in Boyacá. Your father is ill, ill. . . ."

Claudio took one step toward her then. His eyes
bored into hers, and he was just as desperate, just as
wrathful. "And your mother? What about her?" He
glared at her. "Where do you think your mother is?
She's with us in the village. That's where she lives.
She's just as ill as my father, maybe even worse. Who
told you that your mother was dead? Doña Ana Eugenia lives with us, with us, mind you, in the village.
She's no better than my father." He looked at Pilar.
All the blood had run from her face.

"No." She spoke so softly that her voice was almost
inaudible. "No, no, it can't be true. Not my mother."

"I came to warn you," Claudio said, suddenly
weary. "To take you away, far away, before everyone
knows. They'll be talking about her in the village and
at the hacienda. Everybody will talk everywhere!" He
fell silent, and they looked at each other. Their eyes
were large with despair, their rage abated.

"And now?" Pilar said.

Claudio stood quietly, his head huddled between his
shoulders as if he were cold.

"I hurt you," Pilar said.

"I hurt you too." Softly he added, "I wanted to
protect you, and now I myself. . . ." He looked at her
in despair. "You must try to forget. . . ."

"Forget!" Pilar repeated. Her voice was tired, her

face drawn and older. "At any rate, I know what the trouble is. At least, when people talk I will know what it's all about. And I don't have to be frightened anymore, never again!"

Claudio didn't answer, and Pilar turned her horse. She hesitated, as if waiting for Claudio to call her back. But he did not. Slowly she rode away, farther and farther from him. Claudio watched her until she had disappeared in the quivering heat of the rolling countryside into the green haze of the trees around the lake. Then he walked back to the village.

22

There was no one in Lucindo's workshop. In the dark little back room, the hammock had been drawn up to the beam. In the back yard the parrot still shrieked, *"Mamacitaaa!"* When Claudio appeared in the doorway, Lucindo was standing there looking lost. Almost all the animals were gone. He looked up. "Ah, it's you," he said softly.

"Yes, it's me," Claudio answered.

"I got a good price for the chickens and the rabbits and the pigs," Lucindo said. "And I found a home for the dogs and for the mice. But I'm still stuck with the turtle and the parrot."

"Ah, yes," Claudio answered.

"The birds are at Florinda's. She said I could bring the parrot as well, but he makes too much noise. I gave Tito away. Perhaps I'll give the parrot to Alirio."

"Yes, that's a good idea," Claudio answered. "To Alirio. . . ."

"Florinda's garden is beautiful and well cared for.

180

Such pretty flowers. Of course, I can't keep any animals there."

"No," Claudio agreed. He looked around the empty yard. Only the turtle crawled on the ground, and the green parrot walked restlessly up and down its branch. *"Mamacitaaa,"* it called loudly, drawing out the last syllable in a shriek.

"You're living at Florinda's now, isn't that right?"

"Yes, she's on her own, you see. And I'm on my own too."

"What are you going to do with this house?"

"I'll keep the workshop," Lucindo answered. "I want to make a big copper cage for the birds, and there's no room to do it at Florinda's. The room I can rent perhaps." He looked at Claudio. "Your father is going to the hospital, I hear."

"Yes, I hope so, but who knows?"

"And you're going to work for Don Leonidas?" Claudio did not answer, but Lucindo didn't notice. He continued talking. "This morning they went to Doña Ana Eugenia's. To search for the weapon, they say. Not that she would let anyone in. Oh, no! They say she had something to do with the murder of Doctor Cárdenas." He shrugged his shoulders. "People talk. They came to see us too. They took my lizard, and we don't have it back yet. That's the way it goes."

"Yes, that's the way it goes," Claudio agreed. He drew lines in the dust with the metal tip of the cane.

"What have you got there?"

"A cane."

Lucindo peered at it. "It looks like Don Leonidas's cane," he said finally.

"Yes." Claudio screwed up his courage. After all, he had come to Lucindo to ask his advice about the cane. "Want to see something?" he said, and he swung the cane forcefully through the air. The sharp knife flicked out. Lucindo stared.

"*Pues,*" he said slowly and with admiration. "That's a fine piece of work! Beautiful. Let me see." He bent over the metal tip.

"Careful," Claudio warned. "There's blood on it."

"Blood?"

"Yes, this is the weapon."

Lucindo looked for a moment at Claudio, not understanding. Then slowly he realized what Claudio meant. "Well!" he said. "So this is the weapon."

"But I don't know what to do with it," Claudio added.

Lucindo was silent for a moment. "You could take it to the police," he proposed. "Or to Don Fabio. But I doubt that he would be of any help. Don Leonidas and Don Fabio. . . ."

"Exactly," Claudio said. "That's why I came here."

Lucindo shook his head. "You'd be better off if you hadn't poked your nose in," he said. "You live there after all."

Claudio nodded. "I took it this afternoon. I don't dare go back now."

"No," Lucindo said softly. "No, you'd better not." After a while he added slowly, "You can sleep here for the time being, and your father as well."

Claudio nodded. The offer was a solution for the moment, he thought, although Don Leonidas would find out where they were soon enough.

Lucindo put his thoughts into words. "But perhaps you should leave the village altogether."

"Yes," Claudio confirmed. "That's what I have in mind. When my father is in the hospital, I'll return to Boyacá."

Lucindo nodded. "That's best," he said.

Claudio looked down at the cane. "And what am I going to do with this?"

"Well. . . ." Lucindo said slowly. "I don't know." Then he continued hesitantly, "Maybe Doña Ana Eugenia could help you. She's the only one, as far as I know, who doesn't give a damn about the village or the authorities. Maybe she has connections. Who knows? Yes, you could go to Doña Ana Eugenia, although she doesn't admit anyone. That makes it hard."

"Doña Ana Eugenia," Claudio repeated. Doña Ana Eugenia? No, not her, but. . . . And suddenly he knew.

It was almost dark. In the spacious room at Puerta

Grande, Doña Paulina sat in the faint yellow light of the lamp. The rest of the room and the rooms beyond were shaded in darkness. Through the tall windows the outlines of the hills were barely visible, and above the mountains the sky was black. Lightning flashed continually, an eerie blue light that illuminated the hills and shot through the house. It flickered across the sugarcane and caused the shadows to tremble in the abandoned rooms. Thunder rolled across the darkening countryside.

Doña Paulina dropped her needlework and stared at the open door where Claudio was standing. "Well?" she asked frigidly.

"I brought the cane," Claudio said, out of breath. "This afternoon I took it from Don Leonidas's house, where we live. But now I don't know what I should do with it. This is the weapon that the doctor was murdered with. But in the village there's no one who can help me."

"In the village," Doña Paulina repeated. "Which village? You mean the village down there?"

Claudio nodded. "Yes," he said. "La Gloria." The name of the village hung in the air of that stately room, and Doña Paulina continued to look at him.

"Aren't you the boy who used to work here, the one we heard about this afternoon?"

Claudio nodded absently. He was looking about him, his attention diverted for a moment by the unfamiliar environment. He had never thought of Pilar in connection with this large and beautiful room with the ornate furniture, the stern portraits, and those long, gilded mirrors. He always had seen her in an old pair of jeans and a faded blouse. The background had been hills covered with sugarcane, the whirling steam of the *trapiche*, or the dark green of the trees along the rivers or around the lake.

"I didn't know you were still here," Doña Paulina said in her cold voice. "I thought they had sent you away immediately. My son-in-law, Don Manuel. . . ."

The name brought Claudio back to reality. "Oh, Don Manuel, I really came to see him." He put the cane on top of the piano. He wanted to be rid of it, wanted to leave here as soon as possible. "Maybe Don Manuel will know what to do. No one else can confront Don Leonidas. Now they all will believe that Doña Ana Eugenia murdered the doctor." Claudio was becoming incoherent.

"Ana Eugenia," Doña Paulina repeated. She sat very still; only her lips moved. A moth flew into the circle of light and fluttered around the lamp. "Ana Eugenia. . . ."

"The doctor found out the connection between Doña Ana Eugenia and. . . ." Claudio faltered. ". . . and Pilar. He was going to blackmail her, but then he was murdered. That's why everybody will think that she did it. That over there"—Claudio shot a quick look at the cane on the piano—" is the weapon the doctor was killed with. And it's Don Leonidas's cane, the cane with a knife."

Claudio fell silent. The moth still fluttered between them, powerless, hypnotized by the light. Doña Paulina sat without moving, her hands folded over her needlework in her lap, gazing into space. Claudio began to think she hadn't heard him. Finally she called, without turning her head, "Albertina!"

From far away the sound of shuffling steps could be heard coming across the patio and dark anterooms. At last Albertina came into view, looming up against the shadowy depths of the doorway. "Yes, *mi señora*," she said.

"Go and get Don Manuel," Doña Paulina said. "Tell him to come immediately." She sat unmoving, waiting in silence until Don Manuel appeared. He strode into the room impatiently. Just outside the circle of light he stopped and looked at Doña Paulina from under his heavy eyebrows. Then he noticed Claudio.

"What are you doing here?" he asked.

"He has something to tell you," Doña Paulina said, turning her head toward Claudio. "Come closer, boy, and tell your story again."

Hesitatingly Claudio took a few steps forward into the light of the lamp. From all corners of the huge room shadows reached toward him. The blue glare of lightning was constantly reflected in the mirrors.

Outside it was quite dark now. A damp wind blew

from the direction of the cane fields. The night, electrically charged, quivered and broke open above the hills.

"I came to bring the cane, the cane with the knife," Claudio said again. "This afternoon I discovered it. This is the weapon. You can still see. . . . And it's Don Leonidas's cane. He's the one who murdered the doctor, because of Aura. But everyone in the village will think that Doña Ana Eugenia did it, because the doctor had found out that Pilar . . . that Doña Ana Eugenia. . . ."

Don Manuel stared at Claudio in silence. But Claudio didn't say anything more. Finally Don Manuel turned to Doña Paulina. "So it has been discovered," he said.

Doña Paulina nodded. "It was to be expected. A thing like that can't be hidden forever." Her voice showed no emotion. She sat very straight.

"How was it found out?" Don Manuel asked. He looked at Claudio again.

"The doctor who treated her took away a photograph from Doña Ana Eugenia's house. He had it in his possession, and then he was murdered. So the picture was found. That's how it happened."

"Ah, that photograph," Doña Paulina said. "I was afraid she had taken it. I never dared to ask her."

"So she still came?"

Doña Paulina nodded. "Sometimes," she said. "At night."

"And you knew?"

"I let her in myself," Doña Paulina said. "We would talk about Pilar, about you, about the past. Once in a while I took her to Pilar's room, when she slept, just to see her."

"I thought we had agreed. . . ."

Doña Paulina looked down at her hands. "Yes," she said. "Yes, we had. But sometimes it was too much for her. The loneliness . . . life in that village . . . her illness. That terrible illness! Can't you see that? The longing for Pilar. How could I tell her not to come? She had to sneak through the hills at night as if she had committed a crime."

They had forgotten his presence. Claudio wanted to leave, but did not move. The moth had escaped and was fluttering blindly. But Claudio stood there, rooted, caught in the yellow pool of light. In the huge mirror, its shimmering surface reflecting the lightning, he saw Pilar. Her white face and streaming hair wavering in the old glass, she seemed unreal and far away.

"And now?" Don Manuel asked.

"And now? It's known at last," Doña Paulina answered. She sighed, as if a burden had been lifted.

"And Pilar? What about Pilar?"

"Pilar, yes. It was mainly for her sake that we made the arrangements. Ana Eugenia didn't want us to tell her the truth. She felt ashamed. And you and I, we felt ashamed as well. We weren't able to stand up to the disgrace that had befallen our home. We were afraid of the way people would react. We wanted to conceal everything, because we were too proud to accept it." She looked at Don Manuel. "You haven't seen her for a long time."

"No."

"She's changed a great deal." Doña Paulina looked from Don Manuel to the portrait on the piano. The flowers beside the frame, fresh cut that morning, were drooping. "This boy has come to appeal to us. . . . A boy from the village."

Abstractedly Don Manuel took the cane from the piano and turned it over in his hand. "The weapon," he said. "The weapon with which someone has been murdered, and Ana Eugenia is suspected. I have to. . . ."

Doña Paulina nodded. "Yes," she said.

"And Pilar?" asked her father.

"Yes, Pilar! We should have told her before. We do not have the right to rearrange the shadows of the past." She fell silent, tired.

In the humid night the thunder deepened and came nearer. The first drops of rain began to fall. The lightning split the sky, splintered the shadows, and lighted up the room. In its blue glare, Claudio and Pilar stood quivering in the gilded frame of the old mirror. They looked at each other. They looked at each other as they had done in the dark mirror of the lake. Their faces shimmered on the watery surface of the old glass, but no longer did they merge into one image.

Only Pilar heard Claudio when he said, "I'm going now."

He left the room. As he went downhill the storm broke in desperate violence, and the rain lashed the golden sugarcane.

GLOSSARY

aguardiente	brandy
chicha	a hard liquor made of corn
finca	farm
hacienda	country estate
la mula de tres patas	the mule on three legs, the devil
mamacita	little mother, old mother
melcocha	spun cane sugar
mi amor	my love
mi patrona	my mistress
panela	large cubes of dark cane sugar
páramo	treeless, high plateau
pues	well, indeed
ruana	oblong piece of cloth, with a split in the middle for the head
tiple	soprano guitar
trapiche	sugar mill
troupial	oriole with black and yellow-orange plumage
vaqueria	stable for cows

Siny R. van Iterson was born in the Netherlands Antilles, on the island of Curaçao, and has traveled extensively. For short periods she has lived in many different places, including Europe, the United States, Central and South America, and the Caribbean. Interested in writing from her earliest years, she first worked on a newspaper and later began to write children's books. She lives, with her husband and their four children, in Bogotá, Colombia.

Mrs. van Iterson is the author of nine books published in Holland. Several of them have been translated into German and Danish. The background material for *Village of Outcasts* comes from Mrs. van Iterson's experiences as a board member of a Dutch foundation that works in a leper colony not far from Bogotá.